Edward Jenkins, Wallis Mackay

The Captain's Cabin

A Christmas yarn

Edward Jenkins, Wallis Mackay

The Captain's Cabin
A Christmas yarn

ISBN/EAN: 9783337192099

Printed in Europe, USA, Canada, Australia, Japan

Cover: Foto ©Andreas Hilbeck / pixelio.de

More available books at **www.hansebooks.com**

THE

CAPTAIN'S CABIN.

A Christmas Yarn.

BY EDWARD JENKINS, M.P.

AUTHOR OF "LITTLE HODGE," "LORD BANTAM,"
"GINX'S BABY," &c.

Illustrated by Wallis MacKay.

MONTREAL:

DAWSON BROTHERS, PUBLISHERS.

1878.

A. A. Stevenson, Printer.

PREFACE.

CRITICS have often brought an objection
—among others—against the few books
I have written, that "they are written with a
purpose." To *The Captain's Cabin* they will
no doubt object that it is written without a
purpose. And so, like the famous old man
with his ass, who ever since he was invented
has been the stock friend of authors writing
prefaces, I shall no doubt be still held by the
critics to have pleased nobody. But that
makes me love them none the less. If they
speak well, I find that people buy the books
to find out whether the judgment be true. If
they speak ill, all the world desires to know
for itself the reasons for their distaste. Wherefore I wish all my critics a most hearty

Christmas and a good digestion, that whether they be disposed to approve or to disdain, they may e'en do it with all their might.

To my public, always so kind to me in that most touching of compliments to an author or an artist, the buying of his works, I may say, that although in *The Captain's Cabin* I have not had before me any of the definite purposes of philanthropy or social reform which were the chief motives of books like *Ginx's Baby* and *Lutchmee and Dilloo*, this book will not be found to be wholly without a purpose. If it should only make you soundly merry at this festive time, or read you some good lesson of human sympathy, forbearance, and charity, I shall not be discontented. Wherefore also unto you all, my readers everywhere, I wish all the blessings and pleasures of a healthy and A MERRY CHRISTMAS!   E. J.

CONTENTS.

CHAPTER VII.

CHAPTER VIII.

CHAPTER IX.

CHAPTER X.

CHAPTER XI.

CHAPTER XII.

CHAPTER XIII.

CHAPTER XIV.

THE CAPTAIN'S CABIN.

D ING-DONG, *ding-dong*, ding-dong, *ding-dong*, ding-dong, *ding-a-dong!* The great ship *Kamschatkan*, 3,500 tons, Captain Windlass, R.N.R., commanding, had cleared the Mersey, and was running up the channel for the west of the Isle of Man, the breeze being light at N.E., and her speed twelve knots. But for the thud and vibration of her screw twirling on the great shaft in mighty revolutions to the splendid play of a pair of Penn's marvellous engines, whose enormous cylinders oscillated to and fro with an ease and quietness that

2

was almost appalling to a spectator; and but for
the evidence of their eyes, as the green-set river
banks, with their charming panorama of wood and
field and mansion, with here and there the spires or
towers of hamlet churches, and all the other sweet
features of English scenery, had swiftly passed from
view, the passengers would scarcely have believed
themselves to be driving through the water nearly
at the speed of a racehorse—six hundred of them,
with bag and baggage, and some thousands of tons
of merchandise into the bargain.

Less than three hours before, the majestic
vessel displayed from the pier, to the eager eyes of
the last batch of first-class passengers, who were
with much ado embarking on the tender, her long
and graceful hulk floating out in the middle of
the noble river, the Union Jack at the stern, the
pennon of the steamship company at the fore peak,
her masts and spars sharply relieved against a
black cloud, while the sun from its westering path

picked out with a golden burnish the complicated tracery of tackle and stay, of rigging, rope, and spar.

The funnel vomited smoke, which the lazy breeze bore aft in a broad black ribbon, and across the river could be heard the bellowing of the great steam pipe, as the engineer, watching his gauges curbed the impatience of the hissing boilers. The tiny tender, rolling in the slight swell of the river, came bowling alongside with her deck crowded. From amidships to the bow of the giant vessel steerage emigrants pressed to the starboard bulwarks, to watch the embarkation of the few scores of " fellow " passengers who were to occupy the luxurious cabins, and enjoy if they were able the rich fare, of the saloon deck. The canny Scotch and Canadian passengers, who had gone aboard by an earlier tender, and had seen and " nobbled " their stewards and stewardesses, and settled down comfortably in their cabins, and secured the best seats at table, now peered curiously over at the later arrivals, with whom they were to eat and drink and talk and quarrel and vomit in friendly community for the next ten or twelve days. These astute persons had already studied the list of passengers which lay before the purser in the saloon, and had to some extent drawn therefrom their own conclusions as to the chances of a pleasant company for the voyage.

Meanwhile, amidst much uproar, immense confusion, wholesale giving and disregarding of commands, murderous heaving about and pitching down of luggage, screams, oaths, angry words, laughter, shouts of captain, mates, stewards, and seamen, and no little chaffing from the leviathan to the cockboat and back again, suddenly a bell clangs, "All ashore!" The captain roars from the bridge to the tender, "Cast off there!" The steam rushes out with a deafening clangour that drowns "good-byes." The tender, darting off amid a cloud

of waving handkerchiefs and a feeble cheer, takes
away and leaves behind a few aching hearts and
crying eyes ; and then suddenly a little bell rings
from the bridge. A man below lays his hand on a
steel rod ; it moves slowly. It moves! There is
a second's pause, a rushing mighty sound through
the bowels of the great ship, a quiver ; and the
screw, at the bidding of that slight command,
twirls its tons of iron fluke through resisting tons
of water, just like a child's toy-windmill in a breeze.
Anon, with a shudder that thrills through every
heart on board, from the experienced captain to
the new cabin-boy—from Sir Benjamin Peakman,
K.C.M.G., the swell of the cabin, down to John
and Betsy Smith, children of John and Betsy
Smith from Dorsetshire, steerage passengers, who
are leaving starvation at home to risk it abroad
—the leviathan majestically moves forward.

" We are off! " says Sir Benjamin, with a slight
trace of excitement in his tone, addressing his

daughter, a young lady of eighteen, fresh from a crack school near Windsor, where she has been trying to learn, amongst relatives of royalty, the accomplishments of an aristocrat.

"We're off!" says Mr. Sandy McGowkie, of the firm of McGowkie and Middlemass, who keep a "store" at Toronto, where everything a man or woman can wear or use or waste in the way of "dry goods" is sold, to yield the thrifty Scots a handsome twenty thousand dollars a year clear profit. He speaks to a neat-looking little Scotch-woman, with a blooming face — just now a trifle pale — and bright eyes, and a fine row of pearly teeth, which she displays to perfection as between a sob (thrown after the tender) and a smile (meant for McGowkie, who however does not see it) she faintly echoes, "We're off!" Honest McGowkie has just brought this little woman from Aberdeen, his native city, where she has figured for a few short years back as pretty Miss Auldjo, daughter of the Reverend Andrew Auldjo, the well-known U.P. minister. That worthy—having come off with them in the earliest tender, and given them many a word of sober warning and good counsel, along with his parting blessing, emphasised by a brief exercise of prayer in their little cabin—can still be discerned on the paddle-box of the tender, conspicuous by his great height, waving up and down a tear-damped pocket-handkerchief with the ungainly regularity of a semaphore, or a flag signal. For the staunch old man is going back to a widower's home, and to his Lord's work, with a shadowed albeit a steadfast heart.

"We're off!" cries poor little Miss Beckwith, a young lady somewhat short of forty summers, in a dingy grey travelling dress and coarse straw hat with a blue veil of ninepenny net, which she drops over her pale face and moist eyes, as she takes from her bosom a well-worn locket, containing the photograph of a man—a man not handsome, and made even ghastly by the ill-used sun, which often so effectively resents the work of the so-called "artists" who endeavour to adapt him to their vile purposes. But she kisses the glass that protects the picture, and her poor little heart, which has throbbed to many a sorrow, pulsates rudely against the whalebone fencing of her stays—her oldest and staunchest friend in the world. She is departing— the steamship company having agreed to carry her first-class at half price, for I can vouch that steam- ship companies have both consciences and hearts— to try her luck as a governess in Canada. That photograph is one of her brother, a hopeless "ne'er- do-weel," whom she has practically been keeping for years out of her small earnings; from whom she is indeed now trying to escape; who only last night, in the poor inn they stayed at in Liverpool, got drunk, and struck her, for not leaving him the few shillings she had kept over to give her a week or two's chance of life in America; a brute whom she left snoring this very day in a drunken slumber, and all unconscious of her sorrowful parting kisses. Great Heaven! what bloodless and bleeding hearts get linked together in this mad world of ours!

"We're off!" says a seedy-looking man, with a sharp, cold, Jewish face, who has restlessly moved to and fro among the crowding steerage people, averting his features whenever they were glanced at, however casually, and drawing low over his forehead a great dirty-brown felt wideawake that looks fit to serve the gloomy turn of a famous night-prowling poet. Sharply has this man, and with increasing restlessness, been watching the arrival of the tender; quickly has his eye run over its company and taken a measure of every man and woman on board; anxiously he sees the steamer at length depart with its lightened load; eagerly he watches the captain, leaning on the rail of the bridge before he gives the critical command;

and deep and grateful is the sigh he heaves as he sees the skipper's hand rise and gently touch the button which sends the order for the mighty machine below to begin its labours. And now, drawing a deep breath, he smiles sardonically on the people around him, and cries aloud, " We're off! " " Thank God! " he adds to himself, with a quaint and profane stroke of piety. It is the gratitude of a heart evil and full of evil apprehensions.

" We're off! " says a man to himself in the captain's cabin, feeling the first thrill of motion, as he lies on the velvet sofa, and glances round the darkened chamber, where his valet has piled up, in extreme confusion, bags, valises, rugs, sticks, and boxes — hat, dressing, despatch, or otherwise — enough for a batch of officials on a Queen's Commission. " Ha! we're off," he says, sighing. " I wish I were ashore again, I declare I do." And he turns his face to the cushion and lies there motionless, but occasionally grumbling to himself.

This man had the best cabin in the ship, on the upper deck, starboard side, at the stern end of the row of deck-houses, which embraced, as is usual in these big vessels, the cabins of captain, purser, doctor, the ladies upper saloon, and the smoking-room, besides enclosing the " companion " leading down to the spar-deck and its port and starboard lines of cabins. The captain, for a consideration, had agreed to give up this luxurious place for the voyage, and to be satisfied with his great chart-room amidships, under the bridge, where there was every convenience for sleeping, and where he was within hail of everybody. Only the day before the vessel sailed had an agent arranged with the owners that his client should occupy the favoured room astern.

But we shall have gone over the whole vessel before we return to our sheep, so we come back to the huge dinner bell, which the youngest and most energetic steward—like the king of the " ghouls "

in the tower in Poe's celebrated jingle—is ringing
with all the zest and ferocity of a madman. Horrible, jovial bell! To-day every one may call it,
with Byron—

That tocsin of the soul, the dinner bell!

but to-morrow afternoon, driving up beyond the
north coast of Ireland in the teeth of a nor'-
wester, when that madcap villain stands there,
and for five full minutes bangs and jangles that
brazen bowl about with a brutal jollity, and over
the creak of stay and warping plank, and the shivering thud of the waves on the dead-lights and
on the thin iron skin of the ship, the wild and wan-
ton brawl of that metallic voice will sound like the
crack of doom—it will thrill to many ears as if it
were the demoniac howling of a spirit of the storm,
or like the hideous cachinnation of some diabo-
lical cynic sitting at the foot of the companion,
and laughing over the sorrows of the wretches who,
huddled and cowering and squirming in their nar-

row berths, have that horrible sensation of going up
to heaven and going down into the deep, so well
described by a psalmist, and have become for the
nonce utterly indifferent where it might all end, if
the infernal torture could only be straightway and
for ever terminated. — But here, again, we must
pull up our too active Pegasus. To begin, we were
too *retro*spective ; now we are *pro*specting too far.
For the moment, at least, when this hideous jangle,
inadequately reported in our first sentence, startles
the ship, the sea is smooth and the air is appe-
tizing, and from nearly every cabin, with few exceptions, ladies and gentlemen and cads and counter-
jumpers are streaming into the great saloon.

In the broad, long, low room, with its row of
round - eyed lights, its polished panels, gilded
cornices, and flashing mirrors, two tables are laid
out on either side. That to the right, entering
on the port side, is the captain's table, at the top
whereof sit those whom he selects for the honour

to the number of twelve, friends of himself or the owners, and distinguished passengers. On the left is the purser's table, frequented mostly by bachelors, old and young, and by leery commercials, who are married when at home, but are travelling for the voyage *en garçon*—a most lively table, where the purser genially encourages a vast consumption of strong sherry and stronger whiskies, where rough joke and broad story are never wanting; and where, however dark or unweatherly the day, the men come up to the call of the imp with the bell, the strong stomachs of these practised voyagers ever standing out manfully against the perturbing efforts of storm and wave.

Soup is on the table. Many of the guests are seated. Stewards are standing at intervals of every ten persons on either side of the long tables, curiously examining their squads of victims, and forming estimates of the probable amount of the gratuities when the voyage is over. A bell tinkles, the covers of the soup tureens come off with a flourish, their steaming contents are ladled out, and clattering spoons and smacking lips give testimony rather to the appetite than to the good-breeding of the general company. The benches are pretty well filled. There are eighty-seven cabin passengers on board. Here and there in the long ranks a hiatus is visible, the empty chair of some invalid, or weak-stomached man or woman, or of some one whose sorrow at parting is keener than appetite. There is also at first a considerable blank at the head of the captain's table. He of course is absent. So long as his ship is in the channel he will not leave the deck. But to the right and left of his seat several places are vacant. The cards of the persons to whom they have been assigned lie on the table-cloth.

"Where are the swells?" said a coarse-looking middle-aged man, with cheeks that looked as if it was no unusual thing for them to weather an Atlantic storm, and who sat at the foot of the captain's table. He addressed a young gentleman opposite to him, tall, with dark hair and eyes, well-cut features, and a reserved and haughty bearing.

The young man lazily lifted his eyes towards the speaker, and inquired rather with them than by his tone of voice—which was fashionably drawling and monotonous—"I beg pardon. What do you mean ?"

"Why, don't you see," replied the other, not minding his fellow-traveller's manner, "there ain't any one at the head of the table, where the swells sit ?"

"Oh !" returned the young man, quietly applying himself again to his soup. The red-faced man plied his spoon vigorously and audibly. When he had done, he renewed the attack.

"You know, I s'pose, that only the captain's friends and the 'aristocracy' are allowed to sit in the twelve first places ?"

The first to enter was a large, over-dressed, haughty-looking woman.

"No. I am not an experienced traveller. I never was at sea before," said the other, carelessly.

"Yes," persisted the man; "it's a sheer bit of humbug. I've seen fellows sitting up there I shouldn't care to associate with. There is always such a lot of snobbery about these things. *I* prefer to come to this end of the table. It's the most independent, and *I* think the most respectable."

At this moment an elderly gentleman opened the door which led into the saloon from the passage, and stepping aside, made way for two ladies, who, leisurely sailing in, instantly attracted all eyes at both tables. The first to enter was a large, over-dressed, haughty-looking woman, whose features, no longer handsome, were nevertheless striking, and expressive of a powerful character. As she stepped through the door, she brusquely lifted her gold eye-glass, and with a sweep round the saloon, took in the whole company, deliberately, from the captain's end round to the purser, and from the

purser round again to the captain's seat. Then
she turned to her companion, a young girl, here-
after to be described, and beckoning to her to take
the place to the left of the captain, herself secured
that at the post of honour on the right. The
elderly gentleman, who also carried and used
sharply a pair of gold glasses, seated himself next
to the younger lady, on an imperative nod from
the other. We have said that several seats were
unoccupied. The lady again raised her glasses and
read the name on the card placed next to her own.
She then reached over for the card beyond, and
perused it carefully. By a quick impatient movement she ordered the gentleman to hand her the
cards which were in corresponding relation to him
on the other side ; and when she had studied these,
and returned them, she applied herself to her soup.
One card only remained uninspected. It was the
fourth on the captain's right. That one apparently escaped her.

The card at her own right hand bore the name of Mrs. Carpmael, the next one that of Mr. Carpmael. On the opposite side, near the elderly gentleman, were the names of Mr. and Mrs. McGowkie.

" Of Toronto," the gentleman had said, in answer to an interrogatory raising of the lady's eyebrows. " Dry goods."

" Captain's friends, I suppose," she said, carelessly.

" Yes. No doubt. McGowkie is making money —he's a good man of business."

" Humph ! Well, here he is, I dare say," said the lady, as the Scotchman, entering first, dressed in his rough tweed suit, was followed by his pretty wife, who had mounted a bright coquettish little cap, which the thrifty storeman had selected for her from a wholesale lot at the Wood Street Warehouse Company's, in London.

Mr. McGowkie nodded to the elderly gentleman,

3 *

neither familiarly nor rudely, but with a certain sedate assurance. He allowed his wife to take her seat next to the knight—for the party at the head of the table was in fact that of Sir Benjamin Peakman—and seeming not to notice the fact that both his wife and himself were being mercilessly ogled by Lady Peakman, McGowkie said:

"Sir Benjamin, I beg to introduce you to my wife, Mistress McGowkie. She's ower fresh as yet to matrimony, and to sailing, too; but she'll get experience in time."

Sir Benjamin thereupon shook hands with Mrs. McGowkie, with the air of a nobleman condescending to his housekeeper.

"I congratulate you, Mr. McGowkie," he said, glancing at Mrs. McGowkie's fresh bright face. "May I say that you are evidently a fortunate man? It is not every one who is so successful in his investments as you always appear to be."

And the knight's eye wandered a moment across.

to his lady, who was now looking at *him* through her glasses. She seemed amused. Pretty Mrs. McGowkie blushed finely, and then asked for soup ; and then, suddenly seeing that the fish was on the table, said she would not take any soup ; and then, getting quite crimson, sat poring over her plate for a full five minutes, with her silly little heart throbbing, throbbing, like a mill-wheel.

Nothing of all this, except the words, had escaped the eyes of the red-faced man at the foot of the table, who had in truth been staring with all his might. Neither had the young gentleman been entirely blind, though he took his observations with an indolent ease and affectation of indifference peculiar to him. He asked no questions.

"Do you know who that old boy is?" said the red-faced man, a little nettled by the young man's indifference.

"I do not," replied the other, bending over his turbot.

"It's Sir Benjamin Peakman, one of the new knights they've made to the Order of Saint Michael and Saint George. He's a wealthy old fellow from Quebec—was prime minister there four years ago; and, for all his airs, was once a ploughboy."

"Really! I think the better of him, then," replied the young gentleman, slowly sticking a glass in his eye, and for a moment or two glancing at the knight.

The red-faced man was encouraged. It was his nature to bait his company. He hated men who were impenetrable, and by fair means or foul, by cunning or sheer rudeness, he was wont to force his way over any guard, however practised, strong, or skilful. He was one of a dozen thick-skinned commercials such as you may find any voyage, travelling from Liverpool to Quebec or Portland.

"That swellish-looking old woman," he added, "with the great pile o' ribbons on her head, and the gold lorney-etts, is Lady Peakman. She's a strange woman, she is. They call her in Quebec the leader of society. No one knows who she is or where she comes from, but folks tell some queer stories about her. Sir Benjamin Peakman picked her up, they say, somewhere on the continent, long ago, when he was travelling there on business as simple Mr. Peakman. He's her second husband, I believe. At least, so they say. That girl's the only child they have, and a mighty pretty one, too, only she looks too stuck up. Coming aboard, I saw her lift her dress, and she had on fine silk stockings, all pink colour, like a ballet-girl's."

"Humph!" said the young man, taking no notice whatever of the girl to whom his attention had been directed. "You see sharply; you might be a haberdasher, sir," looking keenly at his tormentor. Then, with great *nonchalance*, he proceeded to discuss the stewed kidneys which had now reached the table.

The red-faced man grew redder for an instant, for the youth had hit him, by some extraordinary chance, squarely and accurately. He was Mr. Twopenny, hosier and haberdasher, of West Notre-Dame Street, Montreal. He relapsed for awhile upon his food, and waited for another opportunity. After a hasty struggle with a large plate of kidneys and potatoes, he glanced up the table again.

"La! there's the Carpmaels come in," he said. "That man, sir, has the biggest law business in Montreal. There ain't a lawyer in the province can touch him. That's his wife, with the thin nose and nut-cracker face. They say she's distantly connected with the nobility. I believe she was over with Lady Blogden, when Sir Antony was governor."

The young man having finished his *entrée*, and no doubt feeling called on to say something in acknowledgment of the garrulity of his *vis-à-vis*, said, with a studied drawl, "Ah, you appear to know everybody on board."

"Well, I do know a good lot," replied the other, with unconcealed pride, "but not all of 'em. Now," he said, leaning his arm on the table, and stretching forward confidentially, " there's an elderly man I saw go into the captain's cabin upstairs. I guess he has taken it for the voyage. He has a man-servant with him. He ain't here to-night, and I fancy his seat is the empty one up there near Mr. Carpmael. I don't know him, and nobody on board seems to know him. His name is Fex. I saw it on the boxes. A queer name, ain't it? No one I've spoken to ever heard the name before. Did you ?"

"No," said the other. "I never heard the name before."

He yawned ostentatiously, and turned to address a question to the mild-looking gentleman beside him, who was dressed in a dark tweed suit, and wore a black necktie. This gentleman had been an attentive listener to the loud talk of their *vis-à-vis*, and to the mild responses of his neighbour, but had not uttered a word except to the waiters. He might have been an actor, or a pedagogue, or a parson, or a dissenting minister. His quiet answers attracted the young man, and the most determined efforts of the rougher traveller opposite failed to break up the conversation, which was carried on in a tone that scarcely allowed a word to reach him. So the red-faced man turned to his neighbour, who happened to be the little governess, Miss Beckwith.

CHAPTER II.

IN THE STEERAGE.

WHILE the saloon passengers were spending their hour and a half at dinner, and in that gossip and general canvass of each other's names, appearances, and characters, which always takes place at the first symposium on board an outgoing steamer, the three or four hundred persons in the steerage were trying to settle down in their more humble quarters. A strange medley is the so-called "steerage" of a great ocean packet. Walk a hundred feet forward from the saloon cabins, by the port or starboard ways, past the thin wooden partitions which screen in the throbbing, quivering movements of the Titanic machinery; past the scullery and the galley, where white-turbaned boys and cooks through all weathers carry on their skilful labour in concocting dishes that are not eaten, or many a time, if swallowed, never digested, the visitor from the after portion of the ship reaches, just abaft the huge foremast, the large square hatchway, around which in glorious confusion circulate men, women, and children, of many nations and conditions. It is a stirring scene. Sailors passing to the deck from the forecastle bunkers, or idly lounging about; scullery boys pushing to and fro huge basket-waggons of dirty plates, or washing and preparing the vegetables for the saloon and steerage meals; laundrymen with the soiled table-linen for the daily wash ; the baker's assistants bringing up the flour for the bread of a thousand people from the storeroom far down on the main deck below the forecastle, at the extreme bow of the ship; rough women chaffing rougher men ; children swarming in and out ; in fine weather a lively mob of bantering, laughing, and gesticulating folk of all countries ; in stormy weather, often a scene of abject misery, illness, and squalor.

Descend the iron ladder of the hatchway into the quarters on the main deck. You drop among a mass of humanity, occupying a great space between decks, about seven feet high, and extending from the fore part of the vessel back for about one-fourth of her length to a point where the main bulkheads shut in the hugh area devoted to the coal and machinery, and to a score of varied uses in the ship's economy. The only light this space can receive is from the hatchway down which you have descended, or from the round ports in the rough cabins which line the sides of the vessel, and this only at times when their doors can be left open by the inmates. The cabins from door to side-lights are about twelve feet deep. On either side of the narrow passage, which runs athwart the ship, are great bunkers, one below and one above, di-

vided by rough boards—except in a case where
whole families wish to sleep together—into berths
about two feet and a half wide and six feet long—
very like coffins with the lid off. Into this chamber,
where air can never enter during the whole passage,
except through the door and from the space between decks outside, which itself depends for fresh
air upon windsails passed down the hatchway (for
the port-lights are only a few feet above the water-
line and cannot be opened during the voyage),
there are crowded twenty persons. Twenty persons in a cabin twelve feet long, fifteen feet wide,
and seven feet high, with sixty-three cubic feet of
what is called air to each person, when the hatches
are battened down during a gale, is not according
to Richardson's gospel of hygiene. Families claim
the right to go together. Fathers, mothers, boys,
maidens, and infants, huddled into these troughs,
with their mattrasses and blankets, manage as best
they can to reconcile the exigencies of physical life

with the decencies prescribed by instinct or good feeling. Every day, however, these places are carefully cleaned out, and inspected by the doctor, and not unfrequently by the captain, if he be a good one. Further along the deck, in the darkness there amidships, where a lanthorn is always necessary to enable you to pick your way, you may find the quarters of the single men—narrow berths hastily but firmly knocked up with rough deal boards, when it is found by the owners that living freight is for that voyage to take the place of dead weight. For the single women, a curious mixture of poverty - stricken respectability and indescribable immorality, one or two of the larger cabins are set aside ; and, if the officer in charge does his duty, they will be kept free from the intrusion of men.

The conditions are the very best that can be attained for sea travelling at six guineas a head. The air in this place, even in the early morning, is on ordinary occasions by no means foul. But when the safety of the ship necessitates the closing of all openings, it is likely that the steerage is a trifle worse off than the saloon.

To maintain order in the motley assemblage, to preserve young people from the vilest contamination, to watch a society so various and so rudely cast together, you may as well admit is an impossible task. It is however attempted, and as well done as it can be by some of the steamship owners —by the owners of the *Kamschatkan* and her sister ships. And happily for human nature there are rarely wanting among these reeking crowds persons who, skilled in benevolent work and taught by experience something of the temptations and evils of life, and also of blessed antidotes, give themselves up to the task of mitigating the horrors, the abominations, the perils, of these intolerable circumstances.

The confusion in the gangway, and on the middle and lower deck, upon the first night out

of the *Kamschatkan* was indescribable. A gang
of men under the direction of the fourth officer
and the steerage steward were trying to clear
away and stow in the luggage-room a quantity
of boxes, baskets, bags, and bundles which still
lay about, and which the owners cherished the
impossible hope of retaining in or near their
sleeping-places during the voyage. Loud quarrels,
objurgations in half-a-dozen different languages,
the commanding voice of the officer, the chaff of
the disinterested onlookers, the movement to and
fro of bodies of people, groups of friends, large
families, fathers and mothers seeking lost children,
and squalling younglings looking for vanished
parents, altogether produced an effect such as
might be imagined from a combination of Babel
with Bedlam. In the middle of it here and there
might be seen a few groups of persons who, regardless of the noise and commotion, sat at the
rough tables which were fixed across the deck at

its widest part. Some of these groups were finish-
ing the tea and bread which had lately been served
to them upstairs on the main deck, in their tin
cups and on their platters of the same metal.
Others were drinking off their small stores of ale
or spirits, brought on board in defiance of the
rules, and which they desired to get rid of at
one bout, before the officials had had time to ob-
serve them. Towards one of these groups—which
was particularly noisy and uproarious, and in the
middle of which there was going on, with the aid
of the lanthorn that swung from the beam above
them, some game of cards—the man with the wideawake hat and Jewish face was pushing his way
through the stirring crowd. A buxom young girl
of about sixteen or eighteen years of age, turning
hurriedly out of the cabin in which she had been
aiding her mother to arrange the family bunker,
ran against him.

He instantly threw his arms round her, crying

out, "Now, my dear, not so quick. You're pretty fast at wooing, you are."

The girl's face grew crimson as she struggled to get free, and finding the man's arms were powerful and his manner determined, she gave him a sharp slap in the face, which left the marks of her rosy fingers even on his pallid complexion.

" D— you ! " said he, throwing her off violently. " I'll pay you off for this before we get ashore."

" Yo will, eh, maister ? " said a long, slouching, broad-chested fellow, who, stretched out, would have been six feet one, to an inch, but whom the bending influence of labour had brought down a few inches. " Yo take my caounsel, wull ee, and leäve she aloan."

Looking up and down the rough-clad dimensions of the fresh-looking Norfolk giant, who owned to a friendship with the girl, the Jew-faced man seemed inclined to avoid trying conclusions, and wished to laugh it off.

" Oh ! my friend," he said, with an affectation of

good humour, " it's all right.   I was only chaffing."
And he rapidly passed on.   At the same time he
said to himself, " I'll remember you, young man,
and take it out of you, too."

" Chaffen, weer ee ? " said the tall youth, looking
after him suspiciously.   " Then oi zay doant ee
chaff no muore that way.   Oi zay, Meary, he han't
a hurt ee, have he ?   Oi'll crack the skull ov 'im
naouw ef he have."

" O no, Zacky," said the girl, " I'm all right."

" Yo cum and tell me, Meary, ef ee goes on to
try any muore of his tricks wi ee ; do ee zee ? Yo
just cum to me, an' oile pitch im into the zay ; oi
wull, zure as my name's Zachary Plumtree."

Meanwhile the object of Zachary's wrath had
reached the place where, with the scent of a sleuth-
hound, he had judged that there was some gambling
going on.   A circle of eight or ten people of different nationalities were watching four men who
were playing the American game of euchre. Shad-

ing his face carefully with the broad flap of his felt ·hat, the new comer keenly took stock of the company — then of the players — and lastly addressed himself to the play. In two minutes he picked out the pigeon and the *escrocs*. Satisfied with his inspection, or disgusted with the smallness of the stakes, he soon went away.

CHAPTER III.

A FELON ABOARD.

THE ship had put into Lough Foyle, for Moville. The tender from Derry had brought up one or two passengers. The mails had been transhipped. And now the *Kamschatkan*, bracing herself to the task, was rapidly leaving Tory behind her, running directly into the teeth of a nor'-wester. The night fell black and drizzly; the ship, without a stitch of canvas, and with her topmasts lowered, hurled on by the enormous pressure of the untiring screw, pitched her bow gallantly at the vast advancing waves, ran up their sliding bosoms until she nearly reached the crest, quivered a moment up there on that dizzy height, and then plunging like a sea-mew or a porpoise through the

tons of boiling surf that capped these leviathan
rollers of the deep, and shaking them off her
shoulders in a hissing fall of foam, she darted down
with dizzy vehemence to the bottom of the vast
abyss which the rising mass had left behind it.
Everything had been made tight. The fore hatches
had been battened down; the dead-lights had been
screwed on the engine-room and saloon skylights
and the deck-cabin windows ; the fiddles were on
the table in the saloon, and everything was in the
usual trim for dirty weather. Bad as the weather
was, the watch were busily engaged in securing
more firmly the tarpaulins and tacklings of the
boats, and in making everything as taut as possible.
Scarcely a passenger was to be seen. One or two
brave fellows stuck to the smoking-room, and tried
to be jolly over their pipes and whisky. In the
steerage only one man seemed to be able to with-
stand the general demoralisation. It was the man
in the wideawake. He was sitting near the top of

the companion on the main deck, in the coil of a huge cable, talking to the steerage steward. After comparing some notes about his fellow-passengers at that end, he turned the conversation to the saloon.

"You've a rare lot of first-class passengers aboard, haven't you?"

"Yes," said the steward. "Most on 'em wants to get home for Christmas, you see. It's not a favourite time for crossing, but this is a new ship, and captain's a favourite, and so a good many on 'em have been waiting. I never saw so many afore, at this time o' year."

"Hah! Anybody particular aboard?"

"Well, there's a live lord among the rest. A young fellow, I believe, name of Lord Pendlebury, but I haven't seen him. Then there's old Sir Benjamin Peakman and his wife and daughter. He's as rich as Creases. I don't know of any other folks of consequence. The usual lot, I suppose, commercial travellers, agents, and small trades-people."

"You say Sir Benjamin Peakman is rich? Has he got a valet with him?"

"Not on board this time. He generally has one when he crosses.—There's a fellow, by the way, in the captain's cabin, Mr. Fex—rum name, ain't it? —he has a gentleman to wait on him."

"Do you think Sir B. wants a valet? That's my business, you know."

"Oh! I didn't know," replied the other. "Well, I can find out for you."

"Do. I know sometimes these Canadian swells look out for servants on board your ships."

"Do you? Have you ever crossed before, then?"

"Not with you," said the other, evasively. "Try a drop of my brandy," handing a flask. "You'll find it *extra* good," he added, winking. "It came out of the cellar of my last governor."

Mr. Crog, the steerage steward, highly appreciated the brandy and the joke. They untied his tongue a little.

"I say," he said, lowering his voice, though in the infernal din that was filling the air from the fearful storm without and the rattle and racket and groaning and shrieking within, there was little chance of their being overheard, "the captain's in a precious stew. Just as we were moving off from Greencastle, after the tender had left us, a little boat ran up from the telegraph station there. A man in the stern held up a telegram.

"'What is it ?' shouted the captain.

"'Telegram to stop the ship.'

"'Stop the ship ? What for ?'

"'You've got Kane, the murderer, on board.'

"'Nonsense !' shouted the captain.

"'I tell you, Captain Windlass, you have. Here's the telegram, describing him.'

"'All right,' says the captain. 'Quartermaster, there !'

"' Ay, ay, sir.'

"' Heave out a few coils of the log line there into that boat.'

"' Heave it is, sir.'

" When it was done, ' Now,' says he to the telegraph clerk, ' tie on the paper and run your boat close alongside."

" In another moment the telegram was aboard.

"' Have you got it?' shouts the captain.

"' Ay, ay, sir.'

" Ring went the bell, ' Full speed.' Round went the screw. The boat was precious nearly upset, and we could hear them scolding as we bore away. —Halloo, I say! Look out ; you'll go down the hatchway! "

The Jewish-looking man, who had been sitting comfortably enough on the huge coil of rope, was suddenly pitched over head and heels backwards into the water-way, and with another roll described a graceful parabolic curve, which landed him only a foot or two short of the hatchway, with his shoulder jam against the combing, where he came to an anchor. The steward ran forward and secured him. He seemed to be much shaken and alarmed.

"There, get down again into your crib, and hold on tight with both hands. Why, you've knocked your weather eye, and look like death. Here, take a swig of your own reviver."

"Oh, it's nothing," said the other. "Where's my hat?"

In handing him the big wideawake, the steward took a good look at him.

"That's not the man!" he muttered to himself. "But he's a precious sharp-looking un, now one gets a sight of him."

Any observer would have agreed with Mr. Crog. The removal of the wideawake had revealed a most striking head and physiognomy. A head with an immense shock of carroty hair, which was in a state of great disorder. A forehead, square, receding from great ugly brows. Black, keen, flashing eyes, gathered inward, and completely caverned by those brows. A long pale face, every lineament telling of strength, and resolution, and passion, and cunning. A nose sharp and thin, with a Jewish outline ; a small mouth ; a long narrow chin ; half whiskers at the side of the face, of a peculiar sandy-red colour, which oddly contrasted with the darkness of his skin and eyes. The lower part of the face shaved smooth as a child's. For an instant the man's eyes looked up boldly and peremptorily into those of the steward, as if to penetrate his inmost thoughts. But Mr. Crog had no sooner seen his man than every trace of suspicion vanished. The stranger covered himself again with his hat. One eye was swelling desperately with a blow from one of the iron stanchions at the side of the vessel. He made no effort to relieve it.

"I'm all right, now," he said, laughing. "What

were you saying? Try a little more of this. I can fill it again."

"Oh, I thought perhaps you could help me in fishing out this fellow. There's a tremendous reward offered—five hundred pounds."

"Whew!" said the other, jumping up briskly, but, warned by the increasingly savage motion of the vessel, tumbling into his nest again and holding on firmly. "Have you got a description?"

His face was turned away from the steward, and his tone was one of indifference, but if Mr. Crog could have peered under the dark sombrero, he would have seen on those singular features a mixture of irrepressible pain and anxiety.

"Yes," said Mr. Crog.—"Take care! Don't you go squirming about so, or you'll be off again. I've got it here. The capen gave me a copy of it. Every officer and steward has a copy. It's short, you see, being by telegraph. We was to have waited till the detective arrived by special boat from Derry, with the full description, and no one was to be allowed to go ashore. [*Reads.*]

"A man of about forty-five or fifty years of age, with thick black hair, supposed to be dyed to cover grey, parted down the middle. Large black whiskers, worn *à la* Dundreary, with heavy moustache. High forehead, big eyebrows, black shining eyes. An imperial on chin, prominent nose, dresses handsomely in frock-coat, or, when travelling, in a tweed shooting suit. Large diamond ring on left little finger. Very powerful build, seems about five feet eight or ten inches in height. Good address, and very gentlemanly in his manners. Probably has a wound or bruise on his left eye. Talks German, French, and English."

"Well, *you've* got the bruise, any way," said Mr. Crog, laughing. "It's fortunate I was by, to see how you got it. They're all so keen after the quarry, I'll bet you anything with that bruise you'd have been in quod in twenty-four hours."

"By Jove!" said the other, laughing loud and long. "Take a man up for murder because he has a black eye! You'll be able to seize a dozen of these fellows downstairs on that score before two days are over. There's a gang of gamblers on board."

"No. Is there?"

"Yes. I found 'em out last night. I've not been a gentleman's gent, and all over Europe, from St. Petersburg to Biarritz, not to speak of Homburg and Monaco, for nothing."

Mr. Crog looked respectfully at his Jewish friend. This was the very man to help him to dig out the criminal from the mine of humanity below there.

"Well," replied Mr. Crog, "there's a hundred pounds for you if you pick him out, dead or alive."

"A hundred pounds, sir," cried the other, in a contemptuous tone. "Do you suppose I'm going to share with you at any less than half the money?

I'll see you hanged first. Wait until I've talked it over with some of the officers."

Mr. Crog was quick enough to see that the astute stranger had caught him, and being a man of sense, he agreed with the fellow quickly, whiles he was in the way with him, seeing that now it would be that or nothing. They shook hands over the bargain, and then the stranger tried to rise to get to his berth. He could scarcely move.

"Well," he said, "I *am* stiff! I shall have to lie up, I can see. Well, don't you be in a hurry about that fellow. I shall stay quietly in my berth for a day or two, and listen to what goes on, especially if this infernal weather lasts."

"By the way," said Mr. Crog, "what's your name?"

"Stillwater," replied the other. "James Stillwater. I've given up my ticket to the purser's steward, so you need not bother me about that. I'll look after myself."

5

He crawled slowly down the hatchway, and limped along to the men's quarters, where he had selected the most retired, the darkest, and most disagreeable berth in the ship.

CHAPTER IV.

A CURIOUS IMBROGLIO.

SIR BENJAMIN PEAKMAN, K.C.M.G., was a new knight, but not a new light, in the colonial world. His name had been associated with the business and politics of our transatlantic possessions for now very nearly a third of a century. Hard and astute, he knew how to conceal his shrewdness and sternness under an air of good humour and even of deference, which, if it reminded one too much of the sleek affectation of a cat, bent on a hunting excursion in a bird-frequented garden, was at all events generally agreeable. He was not a handsome man, but he had large teeth, and he showed them with adroitness. He was always smiling. He smiled to himself when he

5 *

was by himself, and when (you would have thought) he fancied no one was looking. The truth was he always saw everybody and everything. He forgot nothing. His manners were invariably gentle and conciliatory, specially so, some people said, when he meant mischief. He purred, whichever way you stroked him, which proves that the feline analogy is not quite perfect. He had been like this from the time when he first emerged from obscurity into a visible and noticeable life. People in Quebec could remember him — when Quebec was the greatest commercial place in Canada—an errand boy for the shipping house of Macwhappy and Salt. It was said that he had come to that post from the Eastern Townships, where many a time he had driven the team that dragged his father's plough. If mentioned at all, that ought to be put down to his credit, for never did plough-boy carry into town a gentler mien or a more natural deference than Benjy Peakman, when he deserted agriculture for commerce. He was a big boy too, and a sharp one. His mother was descended from a family of U. K. loyalists, who had selected a home in the colony of Quebec when, with a sturdy love of Monarchy and Tory-ism, they were obliged either to flee the new re-public, or to fight to establish it. It was by her impulsion that young Benjy, who had received a tolerable education at a village school, conducted by an honest Presbyterian Scotchman, was led to leave the tending of his father's flocks, and try his luck at fleecing in a larger arena. The result did honour, in some sense, to the maternal instinct. Master Benjamin had been brought up in a hard school. He had rarely handled money. When he did see it he appreciated it. His small eyes danced in his large face whenever he held it in his hand. The propensity of trade, of winning wealth, of keeping it, and of making it grow, ab-sorbed his soul. There are such boys with faculties

otherwise noble and worthy. Had I such a boy
I should pray that this devil might be cast out of
him, for I know none worse. I could cherish some
hope for a profligate, prodigal, debauched, or
drunken character ; but the steady establishment
in any human being, by a gradual process from
early youth to manhood, cf the trading soul and
spirit, with all that follows it of selfishness, hardness,
want of scruple, low subtlety of intelligence, bloodless heart, impenetrable conscience, consuming
hunger and thirst after wealth, and indomitable
determination to possess it at all hazards—present
and future—is the most dismal and hopeless per-
version of a God-made nature that it is possible to
conceive. Rather than that, be happy to see your
son making ducks and drakes of his fortune, if you
are fool enough to give him one, and with some
scraps of honour, of good feeling, of generosity, of
conscience, still glowing amid the embers of his
disordered being.

However, this may seem to be rather hard upon Sir Benjamin Peakman, besides appearing to forestall or prejudice the reader's opinion of him. Wherefore it is to be accepted distinctly as in no way referring to him, but as an interlocutory and abstracted remark, for the relevance and propriety whereof there is ample precedent in numerous works, ancient and modern, admitted by all the critics to be perfect both in matter and form.

Young Peakman's policy from the first was like that of the British Government when it means mischief: it was a policy of conciliation. No one could put him out of temper. His mates could never bully him into a fight or tempt him to a harsh word ; his employers, when they swore at him, saw him accept their oaths as if they were blessings ; he disarmed the most ill-tempered debtors to the firm, or its most impracticable customers, by the gentleness with which he parried their rude remarks, and the quiet steadiness and the crafty devotion with which he insisted on carrying out his employers' commands. He was one day hit on the head by a jack-boot thrown at him by a captain of one of his employers' ships who was in bed at an hotel. He picked it up, and respectfully returned it to the owner, saying, "What message shall I give, sir, to Messrs. Macwhappy and Salt ? "

All this was very amiable, and to many persons seemed to be very praiseworthy. And so it would have been, had it been the natural ornament of a meek and quiet spirit. But it was not. It was simply cunning of the meanest order. Twenty years later, when Captain Gumbo was a veteran, and Benjamin Peakman had become a ruling partner in the firm of Macwhappy, Salt, and Peakman, the old man was turned off at the first chance like a mangy dog ; and when he went to Peakman and pleaded his long service and his six children, and besought that he might not be sent into hopeless

poverty, Mr. Peakman, in his blandest manner and
with the smile of an angel, said, " Captain Gumbo,
I am sorry I cannot hold out the least prospect of
our requiring you again. You have perhaps for-
gotten a little incident which occurred so many
years ago, when I was a boy in this office and you
were the senior captain ? I wish you good-morning,
sir."

The captain told this story all over Quebec.
Everybody commiserated him, but everybody respected Benjamin Peakman the more. They saw
that he was not to be trifled with. Sir Benjamin
Peakman was known, then, to be an able man, a
steady, resolute, even a dogged man ; a man who
hid from other people equally his aims and his
manner of working them out. A trustworthy
friend, if it were worth his while ; but a man whom
if you once crossed, he would have his revenge out
of you in some way, and, by general opinion, would
not be nice about the means. But always so oily,

so acute, so studious of the people he dealt with, so wide awake to their weaknesses and so subservient to their wishes, that all the world, with a few exceptions, regarded him as the "ablest," the "nicest," the "altogether most attractive" man.

Hence when Mr. Peakman, then a wealthy colonist and a member of the Upper House and a colonial cabinet minister, was sent over to London to make certain financial and political negotiations with the Home Government, he at once made his way. His deference just suited the courtly ministers ; his ability took those who were men of business. The whole Colonial Office, from the doorkeeper to the Secretary of State, regarded him as the pink of colonial statesmanship. When he had gone away they found he had got a great deal more out of them than they could well defend in Parliament.

Sir Benjamin had been more than lucky in finding a wife every way as clever and as ambitious as himself. She was devoted to the joint interest, and promoted it by every means in her power. Nothing was too low or too high for her to attempt. She resolved that they should be asked to the Prince's parties at Chiswick, and they were asked. In her Canadian home she had been known to spend her mornings in whipping cream and preparing *compotes* with her own hands for an evening ball-supper to the Governor - General. It had always been a mystery who she was and where she had come from. It was known that Mr. Peakman had first met her at Baden. It was said she had been known as Countess Stracchino, and of course that her first husband was dead. It was a favourite joke with the officers of the garrison at Quebec to say that she was "the real cheese." Whatever might have been her early history, her later days were in every way exemplary. She bore children to Mr. Peakman. She aided him in all his efforts. She led society in the ancient city of Quebec over the heads of ladies who were great-grand-daughters of earls and third cousins of the wives of marquises. Every attempt to oust her had failed. She patronised the Anglican Church of the colony, and was, in the estimation of the Bishop, its real defender of the faith. She was omnipotent. Success always stirs up hatred. She was widely and thoroughly hated. There was a good deal in her that laid her open to attack. Her manners were a trifle vulgar, her pronunciation and grammar were not unexceptionable. Her face and figure were neither handsome nor elegant. But nothing could stand against the combination of a millionaire with a conciliatory manner and the spouse of a millionaire with the ambition to rule.

This lady had been the mother of several children, as we have already said, but of these only one survived infancy — the daughter, Miss Araminta. A pretty girl, with a nice fresh complexion, a straight nose, beautiful blue eyes, brown hair, sweet lips, rather too full for perfect form, and a dimpled chin.

Now the Lady Peakman and her daughter had the best cabin in the ship, except the captain's, to wit, the large cabin which was immediately behind the captain's chair in the saloon—at the end of the port passage. Their maids occupied the next room, with a narrow gangway between. Sir Benjamin preferred the inner line of cabins on the other side of the passage, and had one to himself some few numbers down towards the middle of the ship.

It was the afternoon of the second day out. Neither the knight nor his ladies had thought it discreet to attempt to leave their cabins. Lady Peakman in the lower berth, and Araminta in the upper, lay panting and screaming and dozing and trembling, in turns, all through the dismal hours, as the great vessel for its part rolled, pitched,

vibrated, shrieked, and groaned like a vast tor-
mented Cyclops.

"Oh! Oh!" shrieked Lady Peakman. "Maria,
Maria! The—— There! Go this instant and tell
Sir Benjamin I'm dying. Tell him to come to me
immediately. I have something to say to him before I go."

"Yes, my lady," said the unhappy maid, rushing
out of the room with suspicious alacrity, and throwing herself into the opposite cabin, where for a few
minutes she mingled her tears and—well, we won't
go into particulars—with those of Miss Fanny
Ringdove, the young lady's maid. By-and-by she
returned to Lady Peakman, who had begun again
to shout for her.

"Sir Benjamin's compliments, my lady, and he is
very ill himself, or he would come to you immediately, but he dare not leave his berth. He would
like to say a few words to you, my lady, if you
could go to him, in case the worst should happen."

"Oh, the wretch!" sighed my lady. "Araminta! Ar-a-*min*-ta! Do you hear?"

"Yes, mamma!" very feebly.

"I'm dying, do you hear? and your father won't come to me! Oh, I know it! I have a presentiment that we're going to the bottom. Maria! *Maria!* Be quick!"

In rushed the unhappy maid again, and produced that basin which is at once our horror and our relief when we yield to the antic tricks of the bounding sea. But alas! alas! the girl herself was uncontrollably ill. At times like these nature's longings cannot be repressed, degrees of rank are not to be maintained, and mistress and maid mingled their sorrows in the flowing bowl!

"Mamma!" shouted Araminta, when this disagreeable duet had ceased, and Lady Peakman sank back exhausted, "are you better?"

"O no: what is it?"

" Where do you think Lord Pendlebury can have been last night ? "

" How should I know, child ? Probably in his berth."

" Have you ever seen him ? "

" Never. And now I never shall. I'm dying! —Maria ! "

" My lady."

" Sal volatile, brandy, chloroform ; quick, or you'll be too late! Ah! there! . . . . . . O dear! I cannot go any farther, my heart will come up next. . . . . . . Why, where's the girl gone to ? Maria ! "

But Maria had rushed off in paroxysms of a grief of her own, which was by no means a silent one, to the cabin on the other side, and my lady might shout away, for there was no answer.

ARAMINTA. Mamma, is Lord Pendlebury very rich ?

MAMMA. Yes. I see by " Burke " he has all the

Horndean estates, and several county properties. Are you not ill, Araminta?

ARAMINTA. A little, but I try to conquer it. Do you think Sir Benjamin will make Lord Pendlebury's acquaintance, Mamma?

MAMMA. Oh, certainly. If ever we get a chance with this weather. Mind you do your best. It is your first opportunity.

ARAMINTA. I don't believe I shall ever see the deck again, if this horrible storm continues. Oh, there! did you hear that crash? Oh, deliver us! Something has happened."

Miss Araminta was right.

Something *had* happened.

The gale, which had been blowing with increasing strength from nor'-nor'-west, while the great swell of the Atlantic waves came sweeping up from a point or two south of west, had already created in the cross purposes of these mighty forces

6

a sufficiently troublesome state of circumstances even for a huge steam Triton three hundred and sixty feet long. The wind was charged with icy wet, which was disseminated not so much in spouts of rain as in a ceaseless drizzly scour, which sought out and penetrated every crevice in anything human or inanimate that was exposed to its action. The look-outs on the fore-deck, the captain and the mate, who, clad in india-rubber from head to foot, anxiously moved about on the reeking bridge, peered over the dripping man-sails which served for a poor protection from the terrific blast against which the ship was driven with all the power of the enginery below.

"What does she say, Dick?" shouts the captain in the mate's ear; for, in the horrible rout and roar, voice is blown away into eternal space before it can pass an inch from a man's mouth.

"Twenty-eight all but a tenth, sir," shouts the mate, who has been down to the chart-room to examine the barometer. "We're near the worst of it."

The instant he speaks, high up to heaven, right in front of them, heaves the bow of the great vessel. The two men, holding on to the stanchions of the bridge like grim death, and knowing that something is coming, cast an eye through the drift up the long incline of deck before them, up to the farthest end, where for a moment they catch a glimpse of two men, like themselves, hanging on there with desperate vigour to lee and weather braces. Then there is a moment's poise; the whole of the mighty hulk of the steamer seems to be balanced somewhere about the middle of the keel, on the top of a shivering mountain ; then there is a sudden twist of the mountain beneath them, as it throws the vessel contemptuously off its shoulder sidewise with an angry shudder! Down a terrific yawning pit into a sea-green hell rushes the great ship, rolling, as she runs, over on her lee beam, till the boiling waves hiss up the scuppers and into the waterways, and now suddenly recovering herself with a mighty trembling and straining, in the midst of which the huge flukes of the screw are released from the water, and fly round with a roaring noise and a prodigious vibration that can be heard and felt by every soul on board, she slowly rolls back again on the weather beam; and then, with a mighty roar, a huge green curl of seething waters raise a frightful crest for twenty feet above the bulwarks on the weather bow, and looking and moving like a thing of life, menacing with annihilation the two awestruck men beneath, dashes some thirty tons of water over on the upper deck. See, where it sweeps along, hissing, boiling, prancing, swirling, four feet deep from bow to stern, and then finding no ready outlet, thrashes away some ten or fifteen feet of bulwark, and pours back in a torrent to the sea from whence it had leaped. The noble vessel, shaking herself free from the tormenting wave, rises again proudly to her work, and bids defiance once more to the giant powers of storm and sea.

This was what the two officers saw, and they breathed more freely when out of the seething waters the two look-outs emerged, still hanging on manfully, and shaking the water out of their eyes and hats, as half frightened and half laughing they tried to look at each other across the deck, and to shout congratulations which could not be heard.

But in hurtling along the space of deck confined by the bulwarks, the water, foiled in its deadlier purpose, resolved to make malicious use of its assumed right of way. As it rushed round the stern deck-houses, gathering momentum from the upward incline of the triumphant bow and the starboard roll of the vessel, a mass of water was thrown with great force against the closed door of the little gangway at the top of the companion on the starboard side, and of the door next to it, which was that of the purser's cabin. The impact of a ton or two of fluid was too much for the strong brass fastenings of these defences, and in an instant bursting them in, the uproarious water rushed on, and tumbling down the stairs in a green cascade, seethed and gambolled tumultuously along the passages, overtopping the combings of the nearer cabins, and flooding the floors with briny foam. Shrieks went up on every side. Forgetting nausea and decency together, men and women jumped out of their berths, splashing into the cold water, and, dashing out of their cabins into the long passages, clasped each other with new-born fervour for the brotherhood and sisterhood of humanity. Down through the open doorway the fierce wind, finding entrance, now blew cold and cutting.

Ye gods! What is man or woman either in such a time as this? Lady Peakman, having cast off the shawl in which her large head had been encased, presented herself in a good long *robe de nuit*, at the extremity of which appeared her sturdy limbs swathed in long white woollen stockings, with which she plashed up and down in the water, that with every motion of the vessel washed to and fro and in and out of the surrounding cabins. Miss Araminta, poor child, in a vain effort of decency, had seized and thrown around her neck the first thing that came to hand—a short flannel toilet-jacket—and screaming at once for her father, her maid, and the captain, darted up the companion hatchway into the arms of a gentleman who, in very imperfect costume, and wet from head to foot, seemed to have freshly come in from taking a bath in the open. Her screams were mingled with his groans and entreaties, for the terrified young lady clung to him as if he were a life-buoy.

"Let me go, miss, if you please, for heaven's sake! She's coming, *she's* coming!"

Shrieks were heard from the upper deck, and

suddenly through the open door there rushed into the gangway a middle-aged female, with a turban of flannel on her head and a red petticoat of the same material put on over her long robe, which, clinging in wet folds to her knees and legs, very oddly impeded her freeness of motion.

" 'Tis she! 'Tis she!" shouted the man; and breaking free from Araminta, he bolted down the companion and into the first cabin that appeared, locking the door behind him, and jumping without ceremony into the lower berth, which was unoccupied.   It was the cabin of Lady Peakman's maids, one of whom, Miss Ringdove, still lay in mortal terror and sickness in the upper berth.   No sooner did she witness this bold intrusion, than she added her part to the universal chorus.   But people outside were far too alarmed on their own account —thinking that they were all going straightway to the bottom—to be stirred by Miss Ringdove's exclamations.

Ye gods! What is man or woman either in such a time as this?

"My dear young lady," said the gentleman from below, sticking out his night-capped head, and shouting as loud as he could, in a vain effort to rise superior to the horrible racket, "pray, pray be quiet! I'll do you no harm whatever."

"O dear, O dear! O-o-o-o-o-o!" shrieked Ringdove.

"I'm in earnest! On my honour I won't hurt you!" roared the man.

"O-o-o-o-o-o-o-o-o-o-o!" screamed the maid.

The man jumped out of the berth in desperation and the woman went off in a fit.

Miss Araminta, thus rudely cast off, had caught hold of the brass balustrade at her side to keep herself from being thrown down the stairs.

At this moment a gentleman ran up from below, enveloped in an ulster. Notwithstanding his excitement, which was however not that abject terror from the outbreak of which he was escaping, he could not help appreciating in an instant, in all its

absurdity, the scene before him. Poor little Araminta, pale as a sheet, and with her utterly ineffi-
cient scarlet jacket and white fluttering muslin, as
she clung to the side of the companion, was gazing
awe-struck at the apparition of the lady above her,
dressed as we have described, who no sooner saw
the gentleman than she whipped out of the gangway and into the storm again.

Hardly able to suppress his laughter, the new-
comer addressed the trembling damsel.

"Pray, miss, don't be frightened. There can be
nothing the matter. A little water has burst in;
but, don't you see, we should all have been at
the bottom long ago if anything really serious had
occurred. Take my arm. Here, put on my coat;"
and throwing off his ulster, the youth, who was
dressed, wrapped it around shivering little Araminta, and buttoned her in safely, and then asked
where she would be taken to.

"Oh, to Captain Windlass, to the captain's cabin,
please. I'm *so* frightened!"

The young man made no reply. He did as he was told, carrying the young lady in his warm ulster up to the deck and into the cabin of which we have spoken, the door of which was open. There was a foot of water within, the combing retaining it, but he plashed through this and laid her on the sofa.

"Where is Captain Windlass?" said little Araminta. "Oh, please find him, sir; ask him to get me a place in his boat."

The young man saw that she was wandering, and with great delicacy he said, "Do believe me, that there is no danger. May I go and fetch your father?"

"Yes, do, please. Sir Benjamin Peakman, No. 35. God bless you! thank you; thank you ever so much!"

The young gentleman forthwith departed in search of the knight. As he descended the companion he heard a tremendous row below. The reader must remember that all this time the steamer had been pitching and rolling as madly as ever. The water downstairs was running out of the passages and into the water-ways at the gang-way on either side of the main - hatch. The excited passengers had been calmed down by the stewards, and were returning to their berths. The cabins were being swabbed out by boys, who laughed as they listened to the groans of the shivering victims. But at Lady Peakman's cabin things had not settled down as quietly as else-where. There were collected—Sir Benjamin, in a neat *al fresco* costume of which he was evidently unconscious—for he was a man of very particular dignity; Lady Peakman, as we have before de-picted her, wringing her hands and weeping; Lady Peakman's maid Maria, also weeping; and a couple of stewards.

"Base man!" screamed Lady Peakman. "What have you done with my daughter? Let us in."

From inside proceeded the subdued sobs of Miss Ringdove, who, having slightly recovered, had wrapped her head in the counterpane, and was ineffectually screaming "Murder!"

"If you don't let us in, we will break open the door!" shouted Sir Benjamin, for once in a passion. "What do you mean, sir?"

"All right, sir; all right," retorted a hoarse voice. "I beg the young lady's pardon, I'm sure. I have done her no harm. But is Mrs. Corcoran out there?"

"No, no!" cried the stewards. "There's no Mrs. Corcoran here."

"Well, ladies and gentlemen, make way!" cried the malefactor; and before they had had time to obey his injunction he threw open the door, and, rushing out, dashed his head straight into the manly chest of the knight, and pitching him and the stewards over like ninepins, narrowly escaped doing the same trick for Araminta's benefactor, who was turning into the passage, and then he sped up the companion and out upon the deck like a maniac. In another moment, Mr. Fex, for it was he, had darted breathless into the captain's cabin. Slamming and bolting the door, he was about to drop exhausted on the sofa, when a succession of piercing screams from that quarter filled his ear. There was a female in the cabin!

"Great heavens!" said the distracted Fex. "What does this mean? Am I mad? One woman after another! And in *my* cabin too! Pray, madam—— ["Oh! Oh!" screamed Araminta.] I beseech you, miss [he went down on his knees in the water], for any sake, miss, calm yourself. How did you come into my cabin? Where on earth am I to go to? Every cabin is full of women."

"*Your* cabin, sir!" cried Araminta, who was a good deal cooler than she pretended. "Is not this the *captain's* cabin?"

"Yes, my dear young lady ; but I have engaged it."

"Oh, murder! Papa! Mamma! Help here! Mur-d-e-e-r!"

The unfortunate Mr. Fex was more than at his wits' end. He was ready to jump overboard. At this moment a knocking was heard without. There, no doubt, was the young man, who had come back with a steward and Sir Benjamin.

Mr. Fex in desperation leaped into his berth and wrapped the clothes around him. Araminta, who had not lost her presence of mind, jumped up and unlocked the door. The young man was the first to enter, followed by the knight.

"Where is that rascal?" cried the knight, in a towering passion. All his principles had given way under this severe strain. "What on earth do you mean, sir?" he shouted, as Araminta pointed to the berth, and, catching the young man's glance, they both collapsed in hysterics of laughter.

"Kill me! Kill me!" murmured Mr. Fex.

"There is no harm done, papa," cried Miss Araminta, smoothing her hair and looking round, to see that the ulster was as gracefully disposed as possible. "It's my fault. I rushed upstairs in my fright, and this—this—gentleman—was kind enough to take charge of me. I asked him to bring me to the captain's cabin. For some reason or other that gentleman there had left it—and when he came back he—he—locked the door before he discovered me——"

Araminta would have gone on, but Sir Benjamin began to feel in his gouty feet the chilling effects of the water in which they were standing.

"Take my arm," he said, curtly, to his daughter. "I am infinitely obliged to you, sir, whoever you are, for your attention to Miss Peakman. She is very young and inexperienced."

"Not more so than I am, I expect," returned the young man, bowing haughtily. "I am glad to have been of any service to the young lady," with a more kindly inclination to Araminta.

As the knight and his fair daughter left the cabin, the youth was about to follow them, when a muttered remark from the occupant drew him to the side of the berth. He caught a glimpse of the man's face, who with his eyes shut appeared to be groaning out maledictions.

" What, Corcoran!" cried the young gentleman, seizing Mr. Fex by the shoulder, and shaking him roughly. " What on earth, sir, are you doing here? and travelling *incog.* too ? "

" I'm gone clean mad!" said Mr. Fex, starting straight up in the bed, and speaking with an unmistakable Dublin accent. " Where on earth—or at sea rather—did you come from, my lord ? if it is indeed yourself—for I can't believe my own eyes and ears."

" I ought to ask you that question, sir," said Lord Pendlebury, laughing—for it was he. " How comes

7

it that the Master in Chancery is off duty, and at his age, under an assumed name, performing these pranks on a steamer a thousand miles from Dublin ? "

Overcome with the oddity of the thing, the young man threw himself on the sofa and laughed boisterously.

"Oh, Corcoran ! " he cried, at length. "I owe you a guinea. I was lying in my berth as sick as a dog when all this happened, and you have cured me !'

"Whist, me lord ! " cried the reputed Mr. Fex, putting his head out of his berth, and earnestly motioning to the peer to be silent. "You knew all about the 'proceedings,' of course ? "

Lord Pendlebury nodded.

"And that she got the divorce ? "

The peer nodded again.

"And that she got it on suborned evidence got up by that cursed attorney and thief Mulrooney ? "

"I did not know *that*, Corcoran," replied the young man, gravely.

" Fex, Fex ! My lord, call me Fex," cried the tenant of the cabin, in a ludicrous attempt to speak low and yet to carry his voice through the din. " I've seen *her !*—She's there !" and he pointed towards the thin mahogany bulkhead which divided his cabin from that of the purser next door.

"What, Mrs. ——

" Och, dear Lord Pendlebury, don't you mention the name now, darling, for I'm at my wits' end what to do."

" Oh, it is impossible : it's all nonsense ! "

" No, no ; look here ; " and Fex, *alias* Corcoran, vaulted into the water, and shutting the door, whispered loudly to his friend. " You know when that terrible shock came, I was lying here quiet enough, and thinking I'd soon be three thousand miles away from Dublin and the everlasting banter of the Castle and the clubs, when I heard the

shock and roar of the water as it rushed along
the deck and burst in the two doors next to
mine, and came running in here through every
cranny and crevice. I thought we were all off for
Hades, and not liking the idea of going down in
my berth, I opened my door and ran out on the
deck. At the same instant, on my life as I hold
on here, *she* ran out of the next cabin, the purser's,
in a neat undress familiar to me ; and she no
sooner saw me standing there in my own *al fresco*
state, than she began to give tongue like a steam
fire-engine whistling for water—though, by the way,
at the moment there was plenty of that about.

"'Tis he ! 'Tis he !.' says she, covering her eyes.
'Tis Peter's ghost come to reproach me, just as I
am about to perish.—Oh, Peter ! Peter !' and she
tried to lay hold of my arm.

"'Aroynt thee !' says I. For I thought she was
a ghost too, and that may be we had each appeared to reproach the other at our dying mo-

ments. And I made a leap for the cabin. Faith, I don't know what's to come of it! There was a female on deck, there was a female in the cabin I ran into, and there was a female in possession of my own when I came back. There are at least two people to be settled with, besides *her* second husband, who must be on board, for I was told six months since she was to be married again. You'll stand by me now, won't you?"

The earnestness of the narrator produced on the young lord an effect the reverse of that intended. He shouted with laughter.

"Oh, my lord," said poor Mr. Fex. "It's amusing to you, but it's death to me. Now you know all about this, I need never show my face in Dublin again. Well, well, I may arrange a thing or two, and get ove. the side of the ship, for 'twill kill me, any way."

There was just a flash of seriousness in the speaker's manner, and Lord Pendlebury, who was an astute young fellow for his age, began to be afraid the joke was going too far. He sat up and assumed a more sober air.

"Nonsense, Corcoran. I give you my word of honour I'll say nothing about it. The fact is, in the excitement, you have made a mistake. *She* is not on board. It is impossible. Make yourself easy. Come, I'll call up a steward. They must bail out this cabin, which is one huge footbath. As for that ridiculous old knight, and his chit of a daughter, and her stupid maid, we shall soon put them all right. Get into bed, my friend, you are shivering fearfully. How did you get that bruise over the eye?"

Mr. Fex was soon in bed, and the events of the day, acting upon an excitable temperament, brought on a slight attack of fever. His servant being prostrated, as gentlemen's gentlemen and ladies' abigails invariably are by the weather at sea, a steward was told off by the doctor to look after him during the night. This fellow, having nothing better to do than to listen to the patient's incoherent wanderings, excogitated a theory about poor Mr. Fex which entailed serious consequences.

CHAPTER V.

A SEA LAWYER.

BY the morning of the third day the wind had slightly abated, although it was still blowing what are termed "great guns," and the captain, who had been up the better part of two nights, was taking a few hours' rest in the chart-room, when a loud knock, followed by the opening of the door and the insertion of a dripping sou'-wester, disturbed him.

"If you please, sir," said the intruder, "may I speak to you, sir?"

"Yes, Mr. Stackpoole, if it is anything important. Come in."

The intruder was the fourth officer, and he was followed by a steward, Cadbury. They both looked very grave.

"I think, sir," said the mate, "we've got him!"

"Got what!" said the captain, whose brain was a little disturbed by want of sleep.

"*Him*, sir ; the murderer Kane, sir!"

"The devil!" cried the captain. "Where?"

"In your cabin, sir!"

The honest captain burst out in a cold perspiration at the idea of his quarters being occupied by an accused malefactor.

"What, the Mr. Fex ——?"

"His name ain't Fex, sir," interrupted the steward, touching his forehead. "He was took ill yesterday, sir, and I've been with him all night. He's been going on rambling most dreadful, just like a murderer; asking God to forgive him, saying he'd drown hisself, calling out that he'd be the death of a man of the name of Mulrooney—that, of course, sir, would be the detective—and asking his dearest Pearl to forgive him—that would be some wicked woman of his acquaintance, sir."

"Does he answer to the description?"

"Exactly, sir," cried the officer and the steward in one breath. "And we've agreed to divide the reward."

"Humph!" said the captain, throwing off his great woollen nightcap, scratching his head, screwing up his eye, and taking an observation of the two lucky men bobbing there before him, and wishing to himself that they might ever get the reward they were so cock-sure of dividing. "Humph! What have you done with the man?"

"He's still in the cabin, sir."

"But he'll run away; he will throw himself overboard."

"Oh, no, sir. He is very weak this morning. And I've stationed six of the watch, under a quartermaster, outside his door, with instructions to seize him if he tries to escape," said the officer.

"Very well, Mr. Stackpoole. Keep the guard on until further orders. Serve out a brace of pistols

to the quartermaster, with orders to shoot the man
if he becomes unmanageable. If you want to get
your reward, Mr. Stackpoole, you must produce
him, dead or alive. It will never do to let him go
overboard, you know."

Mr. Stackpoole smiled appreciatively at the
captain's shrewdness, and he and Mr. Cadbury left
the honest master to his own reflections. These
reflections were anything but pleasant. He knew
nothing of any laws except those of navigation and
cyclones, and such scraps of land legislation as
particularly affected his ship and his jurisdiction
when in port. The job in hand he did not relish.
If he were to make a mistake he had sense enough
to know it would turn out very seriously for him.
This person, who had given him £12 for the use of
his cabin, he had seen. He seemed to be a gentlemanly man : the steward might be quite wrong in
his surmises. The captain therefore resolved to
act very cautiously. He went down, as soon as

he had dressed, to take the opinion of Sir Benjamin Peakman. The knight was not the best person to have consulted, at the moment and on this particular subject. He had not yet recovered his equanimity, so severely shaken the day before, and was ready to believe anything of the occupant of the captain's cabin. He was terribly alarmed to hear for the first time from the captain's lips that there was a murderer on board.

"That is the man, beyond a doubt," said he. "I assure you, Captain Windlass, he behaved like a ruffian. He ran into Lady Peakman's maids' room, and locked himself in with my daughter's maid, a very proper young person. In rushing out again he knocked me down, and I am still suffering in the chest from the blow he gave me. Then he locked himself in with my daughter, who happened to have been carried into your cabin by an officious young fellow you have on board, and but for the alacrity with which he was followed up, God knows what might not have happened. There can hardly be a doubt about it : that is the man ! "

Fortified with this opinion, which an experienced and impartial lawyer like Mr. Carpmael would have at once discarded as resting on no evidence really relevant to the question of identity, the captain ascended to his cabin, where the unconscious Mr. Fex lay, invested by a small naval and military force. There he found awaiting him the fourth officer and Cadbury, the steward. They had been making a reconnaissance.

" He's lying quiet enough in his berth now, sir," said Cadbury.

" All right. Mr. Stackpoole, you and Quartermaster Sinclair will follow me. Cadbury, you stay within reach. The rest draw up on either side of the door, and be ready at a call."

Captain Windlass, not liking the job a bit, but pressing his teeth together and going at it with all

the resolution of a true Briton, turned the handle of
the door and entered the cabin.   His two aides-de-
camp had followed, and on a sign from him closed
it again, looking sharply all the while at the enemy,
who, whatever intentions he harboured, looked
mild enough as he raised his head and glanced at
them inquiringly.   The dull light revealed a large
head, covered with thick dark hair, a fairly prominent proboscis, dark whiskers and moustaches, and
a bearded chin.   Over the left eye was a black
bruise.   The captain and Mr. Stackpoole nodded
to each other.

The tenant of the cabin, who, as we have seen,
was an Irishman, could not remark the mysterious
demeanour of the intruders without an observation.

" Good-morning to you, captain," he said, recog-
nising the latter. "Are you wanting to refer to some
of your charts here ? You're quite welcome. Faith,
I hope you're not going to give us another fright
like that we had yesterday."

"I'm afraid I am going to give you a fright, sir," said the captain, sternly, bending his brows on the unhappy Fex, and transfixing him with a Rhadamanthine stare. "You came on board, sir, and took this cabin under the name of Fex?"

"I did," says Mr. Fex, quailing before the captain's eye, but not for the reason the spectators imagined. "Here, it's all out now," said Fex to himself, "all over the ship; and I need never look near Dublin and the Four Courts again."

"Is that your real name, sir," thundered the captain, shaking a prodigious fist in the direction of the cowering Fex. "On your oath, sir, is that really your name?"

The man who was thus called on to bear witness against himself had never seen cross-examination conducted in this way before. He was demoralised.

"Ah! ye—ye—what is it you're after, Captain Windle — Windlemass — Windlass — or whatever you're called. What do you mean, sir?"

"Is Fex your name, sir?" roared the captain, in increasingly stentorian tones, as he once again brought his fist in much more alarming proximity to the countenance of the suspect.

" Gracious heaven, deliver me!" cried Fex, sitting up as well as he could. " If you must know, then, Fex is *not* my real name, sir."

"I thought so," said the captain, taking off his cap and wiping his beaded brow in triumph at the admission he had extracted. He sat down on the sofa, his great knees coming up to a line with his watch-pocket, and laid his huge arm on the top of the locker beside him.

" Now, sir," he said, "be cautious! You are our prisoner. Quartermaster, show the pistols."

The startled eye of Mr. Fex, *alias* Corcoran, glanced a moment at a couple of long ship's pistols, large enough apparently to carry about sixteen to the pound, and with a shudder he turned his eyes towards the captain.

" What do you say your name is, sir ? "

" Corcoran, of No. 66, Lower Merrion Square, Dublin."

" What other names have you passed under, sir ? "

" None whatever. Send for my servant, he will tell you all about me."

" I dare say," replied the captain, drily. " Did you never hear of the name of Kane, sir ? Kane— d'ye hear ?

" I did," replied the other, with the irrepressible humour of his countrymen. " He killed his brother Abel."

The captain and the two officers started and looked into each other's faces. Their worst suspicions were confirmed.

" Your answer condemns you, you wretched man ! " cried the captain. " You evidently know all about it. A person named Eugene Kane— Kay—aw—en—ee—a fugitive from justice, charged

8

with murdering Mr. William Philpotts, banker, of Darnley, and robbing the bank of five thousand pounds sterling—is on board this ship, and you're the man!"

"Nonsense!" said poor Mr. Fex, breaking out into a healthy and profuse perspiration.

"Yes, sir," the captain went on. "We have the description here. Stackpoole, hand me the description, and you and Mr. Sinclair stand by there and tell off the particulars as I read them."

"Ay, ay, sir!"

CAPTAIN. "A man."

AMBO. A man he is, sir!

CAPTAIN. "Of about forty-five or fifty years of age."

AMBO. To a day sir.

CAPTAIN. "With thick black hair."

AMBO (Excitedly). Black as tar, sir!

CAPTAIN. "Dyed, to cover grey."

AMBO. Ay, ay, sir!

[" Dyed, ye blackguards ! " interrupted Mr. Fex, in high dudgeon. " It never was tinted with a drop of anything but its natural juices ! "]

CAPTAIN. Silence in the dock there ! " Parted down the middle."

The two sailors scratched their heads and looked quizzically at that of the prisoner. It resembled at the moment one of those useful implements denominated a " pope's head," with which house-maids are wont to assail spiders and dust in the cornices of lofty rooms. There was not the faintest symptom of a parting anywhere.

SINCLAIR. It mought ha' been parted in the middle, don't ee think, sir ? (To the fourth officer.)

STACKPOOLE. Yes. All right, sir !

CAPTAIN. " Large black whiskers, worn *à la* Dundreary."

AMBO. Right you are, sir.

[" Dundreary, ye scoundrels ! And who or what is Dundreary, does either one of ye know ? "]

CAPTAIN. " Heavy moustaches."

AMBO. Reg'lar Rooshians, sir !

CAPTAIN. " Low forehead—big eyebrows—black shining eyes—long chin—prominent nose." How does that strike you, Stackpoole ?

STACKPOOLE. Like two bights of the same hawser.

CAPTAIN. " Dresses handsomely in a frock-coat, or, when travelling, in a tweed shooting suit."

They all look round the cabin. Mr. Stackpoole, with a long, brown middle digit, indicates on the peg at the head of the " prisoner's " berth a suit of grey Irish tweed.

AMBO. True to a knot, sir !

CAPTAIN. " Large diamond ring on left little finger."

Mr. Fex moves his hand instinctively, but the fourth officer is too quick for him. He darts forward, seizes the left hand, and there, sure enough on the little finger glitters a large Cape diamond.

STACKPOOLE. Diamond it is, sir, clear as the North Star.

["Powers above!" said poor Fex. "It's a plot to ruin me!"]

CAPTAIN. Prisoner, keep silence till you're fully identified.—"Very powerful build — seems about 5 feet 8 or 10 inches in height."

AMBO. Every word true, sir! Looks like a young hox!

["Five feet eight, do ye say?" cries Mr. Fex, indignantly. "Five feet eleven in my stockings, as I live. Will ye have me measured, captain?"]

CAPTAIN. "Good address and very gentlemanly manner."—Humph!

["There they have me," interrupted the prisoner. "That and the diamond are the only points that are true to fact!"]

AMBO. Undoubted swell, sir!

CAPTAIN. "Probably has a wound or bruise on his left eye."

AMBO. Left eye as blue as blue-Peter, sir!

CAPTAIN. " Talks German, French, and English."

[" Sorra a bit of German ever dirtied my mouth,"
shouted Mr. Fex, emphatically.]

CAPTAIN. No French either, eh ?

FEX. *Mais oui, Monsieur le Capitaine, à mer-
veille.*

CAPTAIN. Ha! Then that will do. Notice that,
my men, speaks French like a Nantes skipper.

[" Does he ?" growls Mr. Fex in greater wrath
than ever. " Me, that the Emperor didn't know
from a Frenchman."]

CAPTAIN. Outside, there, fetch in the irons!

At these words the unhappy Fex, giving a roar
that shook the cabin, made an effort to jump out
of his berth. But on the signal six or seven men
rushed in, and each securing a limb or a portion of one, the luckless man lay completely at
their mercy, still roaring with all his might. The
riot alarmed the lady who occupied the purser's

cabin. They could hear her giving vent to her anxiety in loud lamentations.

" They're killing him, they're killing him ! Oh, captain ! what are ye doing to him ? " she screamed through the thin partition.

" No harm, madam ; don't be alarmed," shouted the captain.

Poor Fex—Corcoran—was by this time subdued and unconscious ; and the captain, leaving two sturdy sailors under the quartermaster to guard his prisoner, went off to his chart-room, with the pride of a man who had done his duty.

It was soon all over the ship among the officers and crew—the only people able to be about—that the murderer had been secured in the captain's cabin. Hence, when the steward who waited on Lord Pendlebury took him his breakfast at the usual hour of nine, the whole story, with many embellishments, was retailed for his benefit. To the narrator's surprise, the young lord laughed at the top of his bent.

"Well, you are a set of duffers!" he cried. "Go and tell the captain to let the poor fellow off immediately, or there will be the devil to pay. That gentleman is a friend of mine, a Master in Chancery in Dublin, and this is as good as two thousand pounds damages to him! O dear, O dear! Corcoran, you'll kill me with laughing."

The young lord having dressed himself rapidly, his loud occasional guffaws sounding through the thin bulkheads, and exciting the greatest indignation among his neighbours at the untimely mirth, was on his way to the deck, when Sir Benjamin Peakman encountered him in the passage.

"I have only just heard," he said, bowing in his most conciliatory manner, "to whom I am indebted for the courtesy shown yesterday to my daughter in very trying circumstances. I am very happy, Lord Pendlebury, knowing many of your friends, to make your acquaintance. Let me present myself—Sir Benjamin Peakman."

Lord Pendlebury bowed—rather stiffly.

" Pray, Sir Benjamin," he said, " do not take the trouble to recall the slight and very ordinary attention I was happy to render to the young lady. I hope she is none the worse for her fright. I am on my way, if you will excuse me, to my poor friend in the captain's cabin, who has fallen into a ridiculous scrape, the result of our skipper's overzeal."

" *Your friend*, Lord Pendlebury ? " gasped the knight.

" Yes, Mr. Peter Corcoran, an Irish Master in Chancery, who has taken a whim to travel incognito as Mr. Fex."

" A most important man ! " cried the knight, with fervour. " But—I believe—lately—he had—a—a—"

" A suit for a divorce. Exactly. And won it. That is to say," said the young lord, laughing, " the divorce was decreed. He was freed from his wife."

"And he is a friend of yours," cried Sir Benjamin, with effusion. "I have, as you may be aware, a good deal of influence with the owners of these steamers. Can I be of any service, do you think?"

"Well," said the peer, drily, "possibly, Sir Benjamin, you may be able to persuade the captain that he has done a very ridiculous thing, and that his owners will have to pay handsomely for his blunder, unless he can patch it up with Corcoran."

"My lord, I will see Captain Windlass at once. I shall make a point of setting this matter right. He is, I can assure you, an estimable fellow, and no one will feel more sorry than he that any friend of Lord Pendlebury's should have been maltreated in his ship."

"Oh, pray let him not regard me in the matter at all," replied Lord Pendlebury. "But you may perhaps know that Corcoran is a nephew of Lord Summerton, and of sufficient consequence in himself to demand the captain's best amends."

With that Lord Pendlebury ran off to his unfortunate friend, whom he found eyeing his guards in mute horror, and listening to occasional groans and sighs which could be distinctly heard from the purser's cabin.

"Pendlebury!" he cried. "I had entirely forgotten you! Only think of this. Accused, under the name of Cain, of murdering my brother Abel. Convicted of dyeing myself—my hair, my friend, 'that never knew a single hue that nature had not painted!' Cut down by an inexorable law to five feet eight inches, which I haven't been since I was sixteen. Handcuffed by these ruffians—I shall never survive this! Whisper, my lord. Open that small box there. It's my medicine case. You will see a small phial, No. 28, marked *strychnine*. I always kept it when *she* was about, in case I should need it. Just hand it to me secretly, like a Christian friend, and say no more."

"No, Corcoran! I cannot spare you yet. You must last out this voyage, at least. Wouldn't the whole Castle go into hysterics over this! I have sent off the old knight you hit so hard in the stomach yesterday, to arrange matters. He's a sly commonplace curmudgeon, but he may be useful. Remember, you must not claim vindictive damages."

"Ten thousand pounds! Not a farthing less! They've bruised me all over: charged me with murder, dyeing, robbery—shortened my length, and perhaps my life."

"Never mind. If you threaten them with such penalties as that, you know it will pay to throw you overboard."

This argument produced an impression. "I say, Pendlebury," he said, in a low tone. "Do you hear *her*, next door? She has been going on that way ever since this happened. Curious, eh? Is it possible she grieves? No matter, I'll never forgive her."

Lord Pendlebury was a man of the world, but

he looked a little shocked at the coolness of Mr.
Corcoran

"*You* forgive *her*, Corcoran! Come now, that's
too audacious! You forget, man, that it all came
out in evidence—though, God knows, I don't want
to be hard on you—and that it was *you* who were
defendant, and it was against *you* the Ordinary gave
judgment."

"Bah!" cried Corcoran, earnestly. "It all comes
of your ridiculous English justice. You try a case
in six hours, and scamp it, while an Irish Court
would take six days at it, and give ample justice
for the money! On my honour, Pendlebury, as a
gentleman, and as I stand before God, I tell you
there was not a word of truth in the charge. We
had no children, and she had nothing to do but to
watch and nettle me, and I was always more lively
than discreet; but, as sure as I live, she never had
any just cause to complain of me. Her attorneys
were determined to win their case, and they got the

' proofs '—as they call them—but there was no truth
in the charges."

"Whew!" said Pendlebury. " *Tout peut se rétablir.*"

" No, no; she is married. I'm glad to say I'm
relieved of the trouble of thinking about it."

" How do you know ? "

" What is she doing here ? She must be travelling with somebody. That somebody is her husband."

" Where is he, then ? " inquired the peer.

" I don't know. Ill, on his back, in one of the
lower cabins.—Ah ! what's this now ? "

Sir Benjamin Peakman and the captain entered.
The knight in his blandest manner made the
humblest apologies for his errors of yesterday.
The captain more awkwardly endeavoured to
make his peace with the Master in Chancery.

" Captain," said the Master, with a grave face,
" I'll forgive you on one condition. Do I talk
French like a Nantes skipper ? Am I six feet

eight inches? Is my hair dyed? Do you retract these and all other personal reflections?"

Captain Windlass, being more of an honest sailor than a man of the world, did not relish this raillery; but he took off the irons with his own hands, and there was a tear in the corner of his clear blue eye as he tendered his big fist to his quondam prisoner.

"Faith, captain," said the Master, "your method of examination was 'cross' in more senses than one. If you were to transport that huge *corpus* of yours into the Four Courts, and emphasise your questions with those big fists as you did with me, there's never a witness could stand before ye. They'd swear anything you liked. However, I'm obliged to you. It's ten thousand pounds in my pocket. But now I'll pay ye good for evil. You say the murderer is on board. I'll help you to detect him, and when he's found we'll manage with him better than you did with me."

CHAPTER VI.

A VALET TO ORDER.

M R. CROG, the steerage steward, had gone through a good deal of mental worry and physical exertion since the vessel had eloped from Greencastle Bay in the manner he so graphically described to his new friend, Mr. Stillwater. The four hundred people under his care were an unusually large number for the season of the year and its invariably furious weather. They kept him busy at all points. Their cries, their tears, their adjurations, their oaths, their threats, their terrors—all of which he would like to have treated with contempt, but dared not, for these people know how to take their money's worth out of the companies — brought down Mr. Crog in three days from a state of breathless redundancy to one of breathless emaciation, and altered his colour from a fine healthy rose-blush to a tint of tawny orange. To meet the fickle fancies of such a various charge, to soothe, to threaten, to nurse, to cheer, and to bully three hundred people who are rolling about in helpless terror and misery, is not an occupation which one would suppose to hold out attractions even to a performing dog, but there are men found to take to it, and not unkindly. Mr. Crog was ever vowing when at sea that he would leave it, and ever when in port reversing his decision.

The storm which had been driving in the teeth of the gallant *Kamschatkan* for nearly three days began on the evening of the fourth day to abate. The wind shifted a point or two; the barometer, like a repentant spirit, took a turn upward. Hope spread from cabin to cabin, where most of the passengers had been the prey of abject terror and intolerable discomfort. The closed doors and battened hatches

9

allowed no air to penetrate below, and to the horrible swinging and shaking of the vessel was added the steady poisoning of the victims by confined and rebreathed air. It is strange that with all those resources of mechanical science which are available in the construction of these huge floating palaces, no successful means should yet have been devised to produce between decks and in the gorgeous cabins, that most successful antidote to sea-sickness — fresh air. What are electric bells and gilded cornices to a vomiting mammal? What is the healthy ozone of a deck rising and falling between some sixty degrees of variation from the horizontal, to a creature lying below, pitilessly turned upside down and inside out amid the smell of bilge-water and cookery? Give us more air, my masters, more air, an you would have us reconciled to the pleasures of the " melancholy ocean."

The steerage—on the main deck below the spar deck—had been, during the three days, a purgatory in more senses than one. It was impossible to rig up wind-sails, and the foulness of the air below prostrated many a sturdy constitution. Here, however, Mr. Crog held on his way, overwhelmed with labour, which was shared by a stewardess, Mrs. Crog to wit, and by the doctor, a little man who, coming on board a very pale pink, had gradually taken on the look and colour of a dirty piece of parchment.

Unhappy doctor! He is the one man on the ship who cannot shirk his duty, and often the man least fit for it. When my Lady Peakman feels that nausea defies all the coaxing arts of her maid, and all the faint resolution she can herself muster, the doctor must be fetched from bed, or board, or cabin, or steerage, to go through the idle form of prescribing again what has invariably failed before, of trying to find an anodyne for the incurable.

"What do you fancy, my lady?" cries the distracted medico, himself half nauseated by the

9 *

ferocious motion, and by constant observation of the symptoms of the universal malady.

"Something acid. Oh, my dear doctor, prescribe an acid drink — with something in it to support me!"

"Lemonade and brandy?"

"Ugh! Don't mention it!" She motions with her fingers in a certain direction.

"Champagne?"

"Oh! gone long since!" Fingers pointing again.

"Have you tried the effervescent citrate of bismuth?"

"Maria! here, quick! . . . . . . Doctor, you'll kill me. The mention of it is enough."

"Your paroxysms are exceedingly severe," says the medico, who has been observing with his head on one side. He has said so to every one in the ship. "I'll tell you what I'll do—I'll order you squeezed lemon in potass water."

"The very thing! Just what I *feel* I want. Oh!

my dear doctor (hysterically), how shall I ever sufficiently thank you! I *felt* I was dying, and you may have saved my life. *Do* come back in an hour, and see how I am getting on."

" By all means, my lady. Her ladyship must be kept warm," he says to the drooping Maria, and hurrying away, buries himself in the steerage far out of call of the indignant dame when, an hour later, after a temporary struggle with his last prescription, she is once more screaming for the hapless medico. If he turns into his berth for an hour's sleep, he is aroused by a terrific thump on the door.

" Docther, doc-ther!"

" What's the matter? Who's there?"

" It's me, yer honour," says a gigantic Hibernian, thrusting into the cabin a shock of red hair, from beneath which his eyes dance all over the bottles that are rattling about in their racks.

" Well, what do you want?"

" Biddy Maclore, me own wife, yer honour, is

dyin' forenenst me eyes. Will ye come before she's gone clane off to glory ?"

"Stuff! they're all dying. What's the matter with her ?"

"She can't heave no furder, yer honour ; and she says it'll be the death of her sure in five minnits, if ye don't come."

" Maclore ! "

" Yer honour ! "

" Do you see those cards in a little tray on your right ?"

"I do, yer honour."

"They're orders for Bass's ale. Take one, and give half the bottle to Biddy as soon as you can, and take the other half yourself. You're looking seedy under the eyes ; and, mind you, don't you bother me again to-day."

"Thank ye, yer honour, ye've saved her life ;" and helping himself to *two* cards, Maclore goes off to claim the " medicine."

Mr. Crog's engrossing cares had not prevented him from giving some attention to the subject of the fugitive criminal. Great indeed was his chagrin when it was announced on the morning of the third day that the man had been found, by a rival steward, and in the captain's cabin. He tried to look up Mr. Stillwater, who, having disappeared into the men's quarters, had not emerged again. But that person had very successfully concealed himself. He was provided with all that he needed, and he made no requisitions on the steward. He managed to get his tea brought to him by a fellow-passenger, who was just able to crawl up and down again with their tin mugs. Mr. Stillwater had kept his ears open to everything that was said around him during the two days, and this acute listener acquired many a hint of the experiences, aims, and destinies of the emigrants.

Towards the afternoon of the fourth day, Mr. Crog, provided with a lanthorn, entered the men's

quarters on the starboard side of the engine bulkheads, and proceeded deliberately to scan the faces
of all the invalids who tenanted its rows of cribs,
top and bottom.   The men lay four deep, side by
side.   At length, at the farthest end, in the inside
berth of the lowest row, Mr. Crog recognised the
great wideawake, under which, even in the darkness, Mr. Stillwater concealed his face.   The truth
was, he had an objection to the skirmishing of rats
over his countenance.

"Halloo!" said Mr. Crog.   "Here you are!   I
thought you must be dead."

"More dead than alive," replied the other, shad-
ing his face from the light.   "Take away that
confounded lanthorn—it blinds one."

"All right.   Are you able to get up?   The
weather's beginning to moderate, and the person
you know of has sent down to the steerage to
ascertain if there's a wally aboard in want of a
place."

"Bravo! That's all right. I shall get up directly. I've only been a bit lazy."

"I've such a game to tell you of, about our runaway friend. Come along as quick as you can."

Leaving his lanthorn for the man to take to the wash-room, the steward went off and waited for Mr. Stillwater at the top of the companion.

"Come," he said, looking at Mr. Stillwater's improved appearance, "you're all right now — and your eye is quite well."

He then related the story of Mr. Fex's arrest, and of the subsequent *dénouement*. The latter was not so much enjoyed by Mr. Stillwater as the former. However, he laughed at Mr. Crog's narrative, which, being the fourth or fifth edition, had become by this time considerably embellished.

"We still have to find our man. Well, the weather promises better now: it will bring him out," said Mr. Crog.

"I heard something while I was lying in there," replied the other, "which gave me a notion that there was somebody aboard connected with a robbery, at all events."

"No. Did you?" said Mr. Crog, keenly. "Tell us all about it."

"Better wait until I've got to the bottom of it," replied Mr. Stillwater, quietly. "Now, where shall I find this old gent, eh?"

"No. 35, port side, inside cabin. Knock. He expects you."

As Mr. Stillwater went off, steadying himself to the motion of the vessel, Mr. Crog looked after him, with a suspicious expression upon his face.

"You're too knowin', you are," he muttered. "I was a fool to let on to you. I shall have to watch you pretty close, my man, or you'll be doing me out of my share."

The interview of Mr. Stillwater with Sir Benjamin Peakman was satisfactory. The knight, not feeling very well, required attentions which Mr. Stillwater undertook to minister for the sake of a few small coins of the realm, about which there was an amusing parley between the quick-witted knave and the much more able man of business. The latter had the best of it.

"If you should satisfy me," said Sir Benjamin, " I shall probably find a place for you in my house at Quebec. You can enter on your duties at once. And as I don't like your coming to wait on me from the steerage, I have arranged with the purser that you shall occupy a cabin amidships. Get your things removed there as soon as you can."

Mr. Crog was lying in wait for Mr. Stillwater when he returned, and was not sorry to hear that the latter was to remove from the steerage.

" He'll have enough to do to look after Sir B.," said the steward to himself."

Accordingly he assisted Mr. Stillwater with

alacrity to remove his effects, among which was a heavy portmanteau, to his new berth. On his part, Mr. Stillwater was not sorry to get away from Mr. Crog's too familiar observation.

CHAPTER VII.

A MIXED COMPANY.

DURING the night the wind veered round to the east and considerably moderated, and the barometer leaped up an inch and a quarter. The late-rising sun emerged bright and clear from the horizon, and the vessel, being now fairly out in the open Atlantic, and running in a south-westerly direction, sped on through a warm bright atmosphere. The huge swell of the disturbed ocean had given place to dancing waves, which seemed from the rapidly-moving deck to roll along in crystal-green battalions crested with snowy foam. Before noon, the awning-deck, fore and aft, was crowded with lounging convalescents, in every variety of costume, lying about in sheltered and sunny spots.

Above them, now poising in relief against the clear blue sky, now hovering over the flaky wake of the vessel, and ever and anon darting down to pick up some of the garbage which the galley stewards had thrown down the shoots, were huge graceful sea-gulls — the prettiest scavengers in nature. The watch, dispersed about the deck, overhauled the ropes, stays, tarpaulins, and other gear, which had been injured by the storm. A shroud-netting had been rigged on the quarter-deck, to keep off the passengers while the ship's carpenter and his mates endeavoured to provide temporary bulwarks for the large piece which had been carried away by the wave.

In one of the most comfortable places on the lee side of the deck-house (which had by her directions been secured at an early hour by her maid), Lady Peakman sat, propped up by cushions from the saloon bunkers, which any other passengers would have removed at their peril. Her ladyship,

however, was accustomed to presume on her husband's wealth, and on her own superiority. She
looked rather languid. The last few days had
convinced her once more of the vanity of human
wishes, and the weakness of the human stomach.
Her large cheeks were depressed and flabby. Dark
strokes underlined her eyes. A good deal of their
brightness and fierceness was subdued, and the
eyelids had a tendency to droop over them heavily.
But she had caused Maria to array her in an elaborate *toilette*. Over her black - grey hair she
wore a beautiful cap of unplucked sea-otter skin.
Her dress was of olive cloth richly embroidered,
over which had been thrown a fur - lined pelisse
of more than half her length.

Miss Araminta, who had also suffered extremely,
if less noisily than her mamma, was a charming
little picture of a recovering invalid. She lay in
the sun, in a scarlet cloak, left open, and display-
ing an elegant travelling dress of mouse-coloured

matelassé trimmed with feathers. On her head was a coquettish little felt hat, with a blackcock's feather, which suited admirably her fine auburn hair. Her little form, half hidden, half set off by a carefully-adjusted rug of the fur of the white fox, while her head lay back on a soft pillow of eider-down, presented a very pretty though over-dressed picture to any unattached young gallant, peer or commoner, who might be loitering about. The two ladies were lying close to the open door of the purser's cabin. Within, upon the sofa, at-tended by a middle-aged maid of sedate deport-ment, lay a tall and handsome woman, herself of middle age, who listened with half contemptuous interest to the conversation that went on without. Seated on a camp-stool, with his back against the poop scantling, was the knight, reading a novel. His new valet had arranged the stool, with a skin upon it, and laid a small pile of books within convenient reach.

Miss Araminta was a charming little picture of a recovering invalid.

It was the first time this man had seen Lady Peakman. She was reclining, with her eyes half-closed, and took no notice of him. He, on the contrary, having glanced at her an instant, suddenly dropped his face, a habit he had, to shade his eyes, and regarded her with a fixed, keen look. Sir Benjamin, coming up at the moment, spoke to his lady, who opened her eyes directly on Mr. Stillwater's face, and catching his intent stare, coloured, frowned, looked away, and then with a startled expression looked at him again. But he had gone.

The knight saw this. "Oh!" he said, "you were wondering who that man was. He is the fellow I have engaged as my temporary valet. He understands his business, though I don't like his expression. His hair and whiskers are a beastly red."

Lady Peakman made no observation, and the knight sat down and took up William Black's latest

novel—one of those books that have charms alike
for the rudest and the most artistic mind.

Presently Miss Araminta, who had been silently
using her eyes, said, "There he is, mamma!"

A tall young gentleman, in a coarse tweed suit,
passed from the companion, and slightly raising
his hat to the young lady, proceeded along the
deck further astern, where several persons were
extended at their ease, protected from the slight
wind by the saloon skylight and its high combing.

Lady Peakman glanced approvingly at the young
lord's figure, but presently her face assumed an air
of astonishment and disgust.

"Sir Benjamin," she said, "come here quickly."
The knight, annoyed at being interrupted, came
forward, smiling like a cherub.

"Look here, my dear. Lord Pendlebury has
gone and thrown himself down on a rug at the
feet of that vulgar Mrs. McGowkie; and, do you
see, she has the impudence to smirk and chat

with him as coolly as if he were a draper's assistant ? Do go·and tell him who those people are. He will be exceedingly mortified by-and-by if you allow this to go on without warning."

Sir Benjamin was not born a gentleman, and this is said to be a disadvantage which no after experience can make up. He put his book under his arm, and swinging his glasses in his hand, sauntered up the deck to the spot where the young peer was abandoning himself to the quaint and easy liveliness of the U. P. minister's daughter. Mr. McGowkie, who had met the young lord in the smoking-room, was aiding and abetting with admirable Caledonian coolness. Sir Benjamin, standing above, and bowing to Mr. McGowkie in his most polished manner, and beaming on the whole party with his curious smiling eyes and large flashing teeth, said,—

"Oh, can I have a word with you, my lord ?"

Lord Pendlebury, inwardly cursing Sir Benjamin

10 *

for a troublesome old fellow, but thinking that he might have something to say about his friend Corcoran, rose and walked beside the knight, who led the way amidships. When they were fairly out of hearing, the latter said,—

" Lord Pendlebury, Lady Peakman, who hopes you will permit me to present you to her, thought that I ought to convey to you a piece of information. She is, you probably are aware, quite an *habitué* of society ; and I am sure that you will feel that she is only discharging her duty—and—and will accept her kindly little intervention in the spirit in which it is meant ? "

Lord Pendlebury, astonished at this exordium, merely bowed, and looked straight before him.

" Lady Peakman was afraid, you know," said Sir Benjamin, who required all his blandness and all his resource to acquit himself of the delicate mission he had undertaken, " lest you should think us remiss, being thoroughly conversant with our

little colonial society, and therefore acquainted
with all the colonial people on board — as no
doubt you can understand persons in our position
are obliged to be," said Sir Benjamin, apologeti-
cally, with a simper, which did not seem to exert
upon the peer a soothing effect, for the quick-
eyed knight saw his nostrils dilating, "if we did
not inform you who and what they are. Because,
of course," proceeded Sir Benjamin, with a winning effort at a smile, "we know that a peer
would not care to be associated with any who—
though they might be very honest people—were
not exactly persons of any position, you know ;
in fact, quite the reverse."

"Oh, you are quite mistaken about that," said
Lord Pendlebury, brusquely, hoping to cut short
this tirade, which was boring him extremely. "I
rather have a fancy for odd company, and cads are
my particular whim. But, to tell you the truth,
I haven't been into the steerage yet. Is Lady
Peakman afraid of fleas ?"

"O dear no! You misunderstand me, my dear Lord Pendlebury," cried the knight, flushing up. "Lady Peakman observed you were being addressed in very familiar terms by the person you were talking to when I came up—a Mrs. McGowkie— and she thought it would only be right to let you know that she is only the daughter of a Scotch dissenting minister, and that Mr. McGowkie, her husband, is what in England you would call a wholesale draper of Toronto."

"Ah!" said Lord Pendlebury, with greater tact than the knight had shown. "How kind of Lady Peakman to concern herself about me! I quite appreciate her good taste and her good feeling. Will you do me the honour to present me to her ladyship?"

Sir Benjamin was delighted. They proceeded aft. Lord Pendlebury said a few polite words to Lady Peakman about the weather, slyly squinting meanwhile into the purser's cabin at its occupant, who was listening intently to all that took place ; and then, after exchanging a few commonplace remarks with Araminta, the peer lifted his hat, and coolly walking back again, resumed his position opposite little Mrs. McGowkie, who became more lively and pretty than ever. Shrewd Sandy Mc Gowkie had not been an apprentice at Lewis and Allonby's for nothing. He had watched the whole performance with a sardonic interest and a grim sense of humour, which produced curious results on his steady face.

Araminta pouted and pretended to sleep. Lady Peakman tossed her head and turned her back. Sir Benjamin's study of Mr. William Black's charming book assumed an intensity which the great novelist would have been pained to witness, especially if he had noticed that not a page was turned over for half-an-hour. After lunch, however, the peer, with commanding coolness, seized upon the knight's stool, and conning with the air of an amateur admirer the graceful figure and pretty dress of Miss Araminta, made himself immensely at home. The facile knight lent himself agreeably to this whim, while his lady endeavoured, with indifferent success, to run a delicate line between *hauteur* and amiability. She was too fond of governing to endure with equanimity a neat and successful rebuff. But little Araminta prattled away in the best Windsor-school style, and by-andby, when Lord Pendlebury gravely asked the permission of Lady Peakman to give her daughter a promenade, it was very solacing to the old lady to watch the lithe damsel leaning on the steady arm of the rich and brilliant young peer.

CHAPTER VIII.

DING-DONG, &c. Once more that dinner bell
with its "clang and clash and roar!" The
bright cool weather had quickened the blood and
sharpened the appetites of the saloon passengers,
and with very few exceptions they showed up
at the table. There was the captain, rosy and
smiling, fresh from his shaving-glass, in his blue
jacket and gilt buttons, every inch a sailor and a
man. He was chatting with his friends the
McGowkies. Sandy had been crossing to and
fro for ten years, and Captain Windlass and he
always "foregathered" with mutual good-will. Mr.
Carpmael, a trifle sea-green perhaps about the
cheeks, and his wife were at the table. Next to

them there had seated herself a tall lady, who, though past the prime of life, still showed traces of a period when she must have figured as handsome. Her fine cap and black lace shawl, which dropped negligently off her shoulders, vindicated her regard for the conventional custom of dressing for dinner.

Lady Peakman coming in, as usual, late, with considerable fuss, exchanged glances with this lady, and saw in a moment that she had to do with a person probably as skilled as herself in the ways of society. Araminta's dress showed that her maid had been put to some trouble in preparing her for action. The knight in his black frock coat asserted the eminent dignity of the family. Behind his chair the new valet silently stationed himself.

"Oh, I thought," said Lady Peakman to the captain, as she raised her glasses and swept the table with her glance until she had reached the

point where Lord Pendlebury—who, she observed
in a moment, still retained his grey tweed coat—
was sitting, " I thought, captain, that you would
have been able to arrange that Lord Pendlebury
should join our party at the head of the table."

" I should have been very happy," said the captain, with the indifference of a matter-of-fact man
who was *master* of his ship, " to find Lord Pendlebury a place somewhere up here, had he applied to
me in time. But he selected his own seat."

" Oh, I know. He came on board late," said her
ladyship. And turning her eyes inquiringly across
the table, she added, with a curious mixture of
graciousness and insolence, " Perhaps Mr. Mc
Gowkie could——"

" Na ! " said Sandy McGowkie, drily, interrupt-
ing her. " We're no to move, my Lady Peakman,
noo we're settled down in these seats. His lordship may just shift for himsel'."

" The impertinent puppy," said Lady Peakman

to herself. "And after his lordship has been so condescending to him."

The lady opposite McGowkie could hardly repress a smile, which the knight caught and resented. Lady Peakman had not been so fortunate.

"Oh," she said, turning deliberately towards the stranger, "here is a lady who, I believe, has no companion. *Do* you think, madam, that it might be possible to arrange that Lord Pendlebury—a friend of ours—who is at the foot of the table, might be allowed to join us by making an exchange of seats with you?"

"Lord Pendlebury, madam," said the lady, quietly raising a single eye-glass and looking at the peer, "is an old friend of ours—I mean, of mine—and I can scarcely conceive that he would consent to the arrangement you propose."

"The table must stand as it is arranged," said the captain, bluntly, and he was dashed in Lady Peakman's good graces for ever.

The knight smiled all the time, and bowed with affected approval upon McGowkie and his *vis-à-vis*, as they made their remarks. With the greatest ease he instantly entered into conversation with the strange lady about the young peer. Her accent gave him a hint, which he improved.

" He was a short time in Ireland, I think ? " said he, deferentially.

The experienced dame gave a sly side-glance at Lady Peakman, on this incautious admission by her husband that the "friendship" with the young lord was not of sufficient intimacy to have enabled them to follow his notorious movements.

" I knew him very well in Dublin," said the lady, " when he was an aide-de-camp to the Lord-Lieu-tenant. He was so clever, everybody liked him at the Castle."

Sandy McGowkie's under jaw was a study. Mistress McGowkie looked frightened. This was a battle with great guns, and she knew who she thought had won. Mr. Carpmael, with lawyer-like alacrity, turned the conversation, out of which Lord Pendlebury was allowed to drop " like a hot potato."

Lady Peakman had used her scented handkerchief very vigorously, and then applied herself to the soup. As she laid down the spoon, her eye fell on the face of the knight's valet, who stood sedately behind his chair. He was looking straight at her. Their eyes therefore met. A curious change passed over his face swiftly, like a flash of lightning.

"Good Lord!" cried Lady Peakman, and she fainted away.

In an instant there was immense commotion. The valet darted round the table and supported his lady. Araminta screamed. Everybody jumped up. Little Mistress McGowkie was the only one who retained her presence of mind. She clapped a bottle of smelling salts to her ladyship's nose, and dashed a glass of water in her face. But it was not a fit which would yield to those remedies. Lady

Peakman was carried by the valet and the captain into her cabin, the knight following and wringing his hands. The doctor, who had, on taking a glance at her, instantly run for his lancet, now ordered the cabin to be cleared.

Later on it was reported in the ship that Lady Peakman had had a slight fit, brought on by eating too rapidly when in a state of excessive weakness. Two persons were ceaseless in their inquiries and in their offers of help, namely, Mrs. McGowkie and the lady who sat next to Mrs. Carpmael. This lady's maid, an older and more experienced person than either Maria or Miss Ringdove, was installed for a time in charge of the invalid. She gave as the name of her mistress, Mrs. Belldoran.

One person on board had not yet taken advantage of the finer weather to leave his quarters. The door of the captain's cabin, surrounded as we have seen by aristocratic and pretty loungers, remained closed, save when Nick Donovan, the steady-going .

Irish servant of its tenant, now and then entered to wait upon his master. Mr. Corcoran, for he must now be known by his correct name, was not merely kept in hiding by a pusillanimous shame, but his terror at the idea of another meeting—even under more dignified conditions—with his divorced lady was more than he could overcome. On her part, as we have seen, there appeared to be no such *mauvaise honte.* She had gone to dinner ready to face any emergency. When the excitement created by Lady Peakman's illness had subsided, and people, finding the patient did not mean immediately to die, resumed their places, Mrs. Belldoran made herself very agreeable to the company about her. Lord Pendlebury joined her as she was leaving the saloon, and a few words passed between them.

"Well, you have not forgotten me?" she said.

"O no, Mrs. Cor—— I mean—whew! I forgot! A thousand excuses. Forgive me. What shall I say?"

" Mrs. Belldoran."

" Your family name. Of course I have not for-gotten you. What a delightful place that Castle was!—But what changes!—How terrible all this is! Forgive me, I cannot help alluding to it."

" Oh !" said the lady, touching her eyes with her pocket-handkerchief. " What I have suffered! And now, what do you think? Come into my cabin a moment, where no one can hear us, and let me tell you.—You swear you will never utter a word of this ? Well. I met in London a very estimable and gentlemanly person — a Mr. Free-mantle — cousin, you know, of the Freemantles of Castle Doynton. He is permanent financial secretary, or auditor - general, or something like that, in the Canadian Government. And, my dear Lord Pendlebury, do you know I agreed to marry him at the expiration of a year from the—the—you know. I cannot bear to mention the word. The year is just up, and I thought it would be

better to go out and marry him quietly in Montreal,
instead of setting every one's tongue a-going here.
Well now of all the most perverse and terrible
accidents in the world—HE is on board.   Ay!
and in the very next cabin.   I heard his voice.   I
have seen him "—Mrs. Belldoran covered her eyes
with her handkerchief, as if to shut out the terrible
vision — " seen him under the most absurd circumstances, which I won't describe to you."   Then she
began to cry.

"And do you know," she continued, sobbing,
"the poor creature ! my maid tells me they mistook
him for a murderer, and put him in irons.   I heard
them struggling with him.   O dear, O dear! was there
ever anything more dreadful, and more awkward !"

"Pray be calm !" cried Lord Pendlebury, who
was distressed at the feeling she showed.   He bit
his lips, for he knew not what else to say.   The
chance of a re-establishment was gone, for here was
the lady *en route* to be married.

"You may at least be friends again," he said to himself, half thinking aloud.

"No," she said, beating her breast. "No, *never!* I sat in court. I heard the evidence. Up to that time, although I was dreadfully angry with him, for he is a most foolish and impracticable fellow, I never really in my heart believed the worst about him. But the evidence of that Homburg waiter! There was no getting over *that* you know."

"Mrs. Corcoran—there—please forgive me, but I can call you nothing else—that evidence was not true," said Lord Pendlebury, surprised at his own dogmatism. He had nothing but Corcoran's word for it.

"Who says so?" said the lady, vehemently.

"I have seen him in the next cabin. He told me the whole story. He assured me on his honour as a man and a Christian that there was not a word of truth in that evidence, though he admits he behaved stupidly and unadvisedly."

"Heaven help me!" cried Mrs. Belldoran, throwing herself down and weeping bitterly. "If I could *only* believe it! I have never had a happy hour since this horrible thing happened. Pray leave me," she added, holding up her hand and motioning him away.

The young peer, greatly moved, walked out on the now darkened deck, and paced up and down a full hour before he could recover his self-command.

CHAPTER IX.

THE REPRISAL OF THE PAST.

ALL night long Lady Peakman lay in her berth. The curtain was drawn, to shade from her eyes the light, which by the captain's permission had been left burning. Araminta and her maid had been removed to an empty cabin, and her ladyship's abigail occupied the other cabin alone. Towards night the wind, which as the gale moderated had gone round with the sun, freshened up a little, and the comparative serenity of the day was succeeded by a slight rolling motion, which was not however unpleasant. To and fro rocked Lady Peakman, to and fro through the draggling hours; listening to the irritating crack-crack of the woodwork as it started here and started there; to the

heavy step of the watch trampling to and fro to
heave the log or haul tight a brace ; to the jingling
of the glasses in the rack over her head; to the
melancholy sough and boom of the wind and
ocean, that strangely-mingled sound which im-
presses such a feeling of intense mystery and
powerlessness on a lonely soul at sea.

And just now Lady Peakman was intolerably
alone—painfully isolated in her own sorrow. For
a great and terrible sorrow had stricken her.

"Oh," she said to herself, " if I were only ashore.
If I were not shut up in this floating den. It is too
horrible ! "

She was a woman of courage, of experience, of
resource, but she was completely paralysed. At
times she burst into fits of weeping.

Had Maria been awake, she could have heard
the sobs, and the low moans between them, which,
strong as her mistress was, and desperately as she
strove to stifle them, would have way. What was

it that went and came with its gentle and its tem-
pestuous changes through the soul of this woman
—this woman so hard to herself, so haughty, so
domineering, so relentless to others! Something
that had happened that day had awakened old, old
memories, long resolutely buried. The resurrec-
tionist brings up dead bodies : but she recalled the
buried past to life, to a vivid and an agonising
reality. Her past! How much of it had she
willingly entombed! How much of it would she
ever willingly disinter ? She thought of Mr. Peakman, who had met her at a *table-d'hôte* at Baden;
had taken her for what she passed as—a widow
with a modest allowance ; had been struck by her
cleverness and adaptability ; had selected her as he
selected his agents and clerks, and for somewhat
similar reasons, to be his wife ; had satisfied himself
that her reverend father, the vicar of a small York-
shire parish, and his wife were dead, which cut him
free of " embarrassing relationships ;" and so having

afterwards found her in every way a clever, eco-
nomical, indefatigable, and ambitious wife, had
sought to know no more. He learned that she had
suffered a great deal from and through her former
husband, an English adventurer, who had been
made, on some absurd ground, an Italian count.
All she possessed was £200 a year, which this man
had settled on her at her marriage, yet upon this
she had been managing to live in continental hotels.
She was called upon for no confessions—she gave
none. She made up her mind to marry this
Canadian merchant, who was comfortably off, a
man of agreeable address, and, as she could
discern, with a keen business talent. She read
him thoroughly. She knew what she could do
with him. She knew what she could do for him.
And she had done much. He leant on her, he
looked up to her; he affected to be master, and
he was her slave. Or, rather, no. They were
thoroughly one. Either of them would have lain

down to make a bridge for the other to step over.
She had borne him two sons, but they were dead.
This daughter was the one thing which kept
alive their flagging, almost satiated ambition. She
must be educated as only noblemen's children are
educated, and by her marriage Lady Peakman
had determined that she should end her days
as the mother-in-law of a peer. They had
visited England in the summer, expressly to take
Araminta home, in order that she might first trot
over the course of provincial society. Besides,
there were not seldom stray aristocrats in Canada.
Away from the surroundings of the bewildering
society of London, not a few of these wandering
first-class meteors had been caught by provincial
maidens. The party were now travelling to spend
their Christmas at their splendid mansion near
Quebec. The truth was, Lady Peakman had heard
of Lord Pendlebury's intention to visit Canada, to
pass the winter with the Governor-General. She

had taken the pains to discover that he sailed in the *Kamschatkan*, and on the twelfth of December, and had arranged her plans accordingly.

But all her pretty designs, all those bright mysterious hopes that seem with the death of nature to grow livelier in men's hearts under the blessed influences of the coming Christmas time, were chilled and killed at the instant when Lady Peakman's eyes met those of Mr. Stillwater.

Under all his disguises she recognised who that man was. She had been simply startled by the first glance at him on deck. But she had persuaded herself that there must be some mistake. The horrible red hair and whiskers, the tinted eyebrows, the smooth-shaven face, these were all strange to her. The nose was pinched, there were crows'-feet from the corners of the eyes. The brows had become knotted and ferocious. The lips were withered and drawn. But those eyes, there was no mistaking them, when they had opened fully on hers—when they came out as it were from their cunning hiding-places under the deep brows, and showed themselves in all their deadly brilliancy. He was alive, that she thought had been dead, and he brought with him from the dead all that she thought had been buried with him—the shame, the sin, the sorrows, the hideous incidents of their so-called "married life."

She was in an agony.

Latterly religion had been something more than a mere fashion to her. As her dresses increased in girth and her face became a more difficult problem for her lady's maid, the conviction that there was another world began to weigh upon her. The discovery of the loss of physical grace is very often the first impulsion towards the grace that is heavenly. She found a pleasure in Gregorian music, in a sentimental, well-tailored, well-millinered, well-upholstered, well-embossed service. And in the anguish of this night she strove to pray

—Let pity wait without during those solemn mysteries.

At length she felt an irresistible impulse. Her brain was fevered. It seemed on fire. She told herself that the bold course was the best. She would go now, and see this man. She did not know where he was, nor had she determined what to do — but no matter. She must move. She could not lie there any longer.

Rising from the berth—staggering from weakness and the ship's motion—she threw around her a handsome flannel robe, that lay there ready for use. She turned to the door. But at the instant— it opened of itself slowly, softly, and a figure with the rapidity of a snake glided in, and, closing it, stood before her. It was he.

It was he, as she had seen him long years ago, only aged by time and crime, and shorn of his trim moustache and gay imperial. His black hair, parted in the middle, waved above his forehead. His whiskers were dark as before.

When he saw her up and dressed, a smile transiently stirred his features and disappeared, as a sickly gleam of sunlight fitfully darts along the black face of a cloud and leaves it all gloom again.

She did not utter a word. She stood there, struggling to be mistress of herself, to call back the power that once she had of half holding this man at bay. But she was not able to recover it. She staggered, and sank upon the end of the sofa, as far away from him as possible, and hid his face from her sight with both hands. There cowering, she spoke *at* him, but not *to* him.

"What do you want? Where have you come from?"

"Silence!" he said, through his teeth.

"*First*," he whispered, "I lock the door.

"*Second*, if you speak above your breath again, neither of us leaves this cabin alive.

"*Third*, don't be a fool, don't faint, don't jib,

don't try any of your damned tricks.   Answer my
questions.   I know all about you.   I spotted you
yesterday morning.   You are a clever woman.   The
cleverest woman I ever saw.   I never admired you
as I do now."

She shuddered.

" If I had had your steadiness of purpose, your
devilish ingenuity, and your self-control, by —— I
don't know what I might not have been."

She kept her face covered, her shoulder turned ;
but now, in the desperate emergency, she was growing cooler, as he became more excited.   Her old
genius, a wicked one, was coming back.   Could
she outwit this villain ?

"You thought I was dead," he went on.   "It
suited my game to be dead for awhile.   I was married again, like you, to a South American woman,
and I had an account of my death put into Galig-
nani.   You saw it, no doubt.—I'm in luck," he said,
bitterly.   "I came on board this ship a runaway

and a pauper, not knowing that I should find the means of a handsome independence!"

"Well, what is it you want?" she said. "Money, of course."

"Not so loud, woman, do you hear?" He clicked the lock of a pistol.

"You fool," she said, rising suddenly and facing him, with all the old fire in her eyes. "Shoot me now, if you dare! Don't I know, you wretched coward, that you love that cursed life of yours too well to risk it for good or evil?"

She had gained a great deal in moral force and dignity during the years that had separated her from him, and it told on his low dog's spirit with astonishing effect. His eye fell, and the pistol lay listless in his hand.

"Are you going to fire?" she said, pursuing her advantage. It was a desperate game. "Put up the pistol, or I shall call out," she added. He slipped it into his pocket, giving her at the same time a glance of terrible ferocity.

"There are quieter ways of doing it, madam," he said, with a cool sneer that made her shudder.

"Come," she said, sitting down, and looking away from him again. "Tell me what it is you want? What do you wish me to do?"

"Exactly," he said. "Let us come to business. Your so-called husband is a millionaire?"

"He is pretty well off."

"He can afford to pay handsomely, at all events, to save himself from a blasted name. That girl is *his* daughter, do you say?"

He said this with a malicious emphasis.

She turned and looked him straight in the face.

"She *is* his daughter." She spoke a little warmly.

"Hush! Let us arrange the matter quietly. I knew you were a woman of business, and I have considered what is the least I can manage to live upon and hold my tongue. Have you any money of your own?"

"Go on. I shall answer no questions."

"All right. You will have to tell *him* then. I must have ten thousand pounds down, and fifteen hundred a year properly secured for the rest of my life."

"Is that all ?" she said, mockingly.

The man struggled hard against the ferocious impulse that was within him to rush upon her and strangle her. Then he said, calmly, "I see I was a fool to come to you. I should have opened negotiations with *him*. I will go to him now. Excuse me for locking you in."

"Stay. I will undertake that you shall have your terms."

"Have you a jewel-case ?"

"Yes."

"Give it to me. No doubt it is well filled. It shall be security. If the money is paid within a week of our landing, you will get it back unopened."

She hesitated. "There are private letters in it."

"So much the better," quoth he. "You will want to get them back again. Now, where is it?"

She pointed under her berth, where it was hidden away. He took it up.

"Now," he said, "I must be off. You will never see me again in this rig. I run a tremendous risk in taking it on. But I was anxious to make you sure of your man. There are five hundred pounds upon my head now. It is understood we take no notice of each other. I shall do my best for the old governor, as he is going to be so good to me. When you have settled it with him, give me the tip how it is to be carried out. Good-night, my dear!"

Lady Peakman did not hear him. Her face was buried in her hands. A severe reaction from the c.r   ort she had made in this terrible interview had set in.

He slipped away like a guilty night-bird. Before stepping out from the narrow gangway between the cabins, he listened up and down the dark passage. At the instant eight bells struck, and he heard the whistle of the boatswain calling out the watch. He glided along swiftly towards his cabin, which was, as we have seen, amidships, just opposite the engines. He had not cleared the cabin passage, and still had to cross the lighted space by the main hatch, when he heard steps. A gang of sailors were getting out the hose to swill and swab the decks. Some of the stewards and galley-boys had also turned out, to begin the preparations for the day's life of the little floating town.

"I must make a run for it," he muttered to himself, as he darted across the lighted opening which lay between him and his berth. He rushed into the arms of a sailor who was coming along the passage way from the forecastle.

"Avast there, shipmate!" cried the man. "Where are you driving to?"

"Oh!" replied Mr. Stillwater, "I have been at-

tending to old Peakman, and it's so precious cold,
1 was hurrying to get into my berth."

The sailor made way for him, and Mr. Stillwater,
reaching his cabin, shut and secured the door. He
was angry and flustered.

"To think I should have met that cursed ship-
swab," he said. "And that I should have been
such a fool as to tell him who I was."

CHAPTER X.

A BOW SHOT AT A VENTURE.

THE morning of Tuesday broke dark and lowering. A chill came up out of the east with the sun and wind. The breeze was favourable, and the vessel dashed through the water, steadied by the sails which had been crowded on to aid the steam. Many passengers thronged the deck, not lounging about, but wrapped up in furs and woollens, taking vigorous exercise. The sea had changed its bright fresh hue of yesterday. It was now of a dull lead colour. The wind and the light swell running in each other's teeth, the roughened waves lapped up in dingy hillocks, the peaks of which were broken by the breeze into crisp white combs of spray. Against the inky background of the sky the stormy-petrels darted about, and the white gulls, uttering joyous screams, wheeled round the stern of the steamer in powerful and graceful gyrations.

Lord Pendlebury, fresh from a good night's rest, the morning's *douche* from the hose, and a lazy breakfast in bed, having taken a few turns in the bracing air, knocked smartly at the door of the captain's cabin, and, upon a call from within, entered.

"Ha, Corcoran!" he said, speaking loud and cheerily, "are you never going to turn out? We shall have nothing but your body to land ashore, unless indeed you prefer a sea burial."

"The difficulty about that," replied Mr. Corcoran, "as the American said, is that your friends don't exactly know where to erect the gravestone. But," he added, sadly, "what matters it? What have I to live for? I should be content to let this voyage be my last."

"Oh, nonsense, man," cried the peer. "Life has compensation for everything with men who are busy and honest. You are getting dyspeptic in that berth. Turn out, and take some air. Do you know," he said, in a lower tone, "*she's* nothing like so bad as you are."

"Humph!" sighed Corcoran.

"She is not happy, either."

"Humph!" again said the Master in Chancery. "Serve her right! What is she doing on board here?"

"*She is on her way to Canada, to get married,*" replied the young lord, with studied emphasis and deliberation.

"To get married!" shouted the Master, jumping up, at the imminent risk of sending his nightcapped head through the light poop-deck above it, while he threw his legs out over the side of his berth. "*She* going to get married?"

Lord Pendlebury, unable to contain himself,

laughed immoderately. A faint echo came from the adjacent cabin.

"Ah! I see, you're joking!" cried Mr. Corcoran, beginning to draw in again.

"On my honour, it's true," replied the peer, recovering his gravity. "The happy substitute is to meet her at Portland, and they will be married before Christmas Day."

"Will they?" cried Mr. Corcoran, in a tone of thunder, as he slipped out of bed with extraordinary alacrity. "Give me my trousers!"

A silvery laugh again in the purser's cabin. Mr. Corcoran blushed and looked foolish.

"Stop!" said the young lord, highly delighted. "Remember, my dear Corcoran, whatever steps you propose to take, you have plenty of time. We are only five days out, and we shall be lucky indeed if we get in under seven more. Let me send you your servant, and then I shall be at your disposal."

In three-quarters of an hour the mysterious Mr.

Fex appeared on deck, walking arm-in-arm with Lord Pendlebury.

The red-faced man of the dinner table was sitting in the smoking-room, exchanging vulgar confidences with some other people of his own sort. He had been relating a cock-and-bull story of the manner in which he had " taken down " the young peer, in a conversation at the foot of the table.

" There he is now ! " he suddenly exclaimed, pointing with the stem of his pipe, " talking to that Mr. Fex who is in the captain's cabin. The first time the man has shown up since his arrest. What a lark that was ! They say the man came aboard here under a false name, but I haven't been able to find out what his real one is. I believe old Peakman knows, but he is such a snob— you can never get anything out of him. He and that old duchess keep themselves as close as weasels."

" Is dere not some story about dis Lady Peakman?" said Mr. Weiss, a German tobacconist of Kingston. "Vas she not an actress before he married her?"

"O no!" replied the red-faced man. "Nothing so good as that. They said her husband was an Italian count, name of Stracchino."

"Stracchino!" cried the German. "A Prince of Milan, I suppose. Eh? Ha! Ha! It is a name that ought to smell—vot you call stink—at all events."

Mr. Weiss's joke was addressed to an audience to whom Gorgonzola and its magnificent flavour were alike unknown. But the red-faced man took the point, though he could not understand the joke.

"Well," he said, "if all they say is true, it did stink considerably in all the gambling-places in Europe. But Madame is clever. She never lets out anything, and it is so long ago, that inquiries are useless."

"Vell," said Mr. Weiss. "Vy vould you inquire?

Is not she vell living now? and vy should you or I
or any von else vant to trouble ze poor lady?"

Mr. Weiss, who was a man of some weight, sat
puffing at his meerschaum, and his words, having
a taste of honesty and good feeling in them, rather
depressed the malicious energy of the red‑faced
man.

The topic was changed by Mr. Turton, the editor
of a low Ottawa newspaper, returning from his first
visit to the "old country," on what Americans call
a "dead head" trip extracted from the owners
of the *Kamschatkan.* He spoke in a horrible tone,
which was neither Yankee, nor Irish, nor Scotch,
but a successful compound of the most vulgar ele‑
ments of all three.

"Well, sirr! Never mind the old lady. Though
I'm of opinion that everybody's sins should be
brought out square, and shown up, for the good of
society in general, and of the folks themselves in
particular." He puffed the smoke from under a

scrubby moustache of a dirty clay colour, and looked round on the assembled witenagemote of Canadian counter-jumpers. "But, lookee here! Has any one heard what they are doing to discover this murderer they say they have on board?"

No one had any news.

"Well, I've been doing a little detection on my own hook, down in the steerage——"

"And you have found de man!" said Mr. Weiss, with great gravity removing his pipe to utter the words.

"*I* did'nt say so, sirr!" cried the other, annoyed. "But, if he is aboard—which I don't believe—he is among a troop of German gamblers I've spotted in the steerage."

The company laughed at Mr. Weiss, who went on puffing away, with perfectly steady features. Then deliberately removing his pipe, he said, "Den I do not give a cent for your discovery."

"I'll bet you ten dollars I'll find him!" cried the

nettled journalist. He spoke in haste, and unadvisedly.

"Do-one," said the German, gravely. "Ve vill
at vonce de money shtake. Dere is my ten dollars."
And he drew out of a greasy pocket-book two five-
dollar notes.

"I haven't any Canadian money about me, I
guess," answered the editor, shoving his hands
ostentatiously into all his pockets, out of which,
as he had been able to anticipate, nothing was
evolved. "You'll have to trust me."

"No," said the German, with a prolonged and
exasperating intonation, as he restored his money
to its case. "I nevare trustish a Canadian editor.
Dare is von bill of sixty dollar of see-gar, dat vas
all smoke up by de editor of de 'Toronto Scalper,'
but for me it all end in de smoke. He offer me
to take it in advertising, but I tell him to advertise
in his paper von whole ten years vas not for me
von customer more."

The laugh was turned against the journalist, who registered a vow that one of the earliest numbers of his paper, after his return, should contain a letter from Kingston, alluding in scathing terms to the return of Mr. Weiss, the German Jew, from his native Hamburgh, with a consignment of bad tobacco and German cigars, which he was palming off on a trustful public for genuine Havanna.

A few minutes later Lord Pendlebury again passed the smoking-room door. He had left Mr. Corcoran chatting with the captain. The red-faced man slipped out of the cabin and approached the peer as he stood near the wheel-house.

"My lord," he said, taking off his hat, "I hope your lordship will permit me to offer my humblest apologies for any rudeness I may have committed in ignorance of your lordship's rank, when speaking to you at table?"

"Oh, I was not aware of anything, Mr. ——"

"Stretcher, my lord. Your lordship will allow me to hand you my card. One of the best shops in Montreal, for all that a gentleman can need your lordship, and I shall feel deeply honoured by your distinguished patronage, my lord."

"Oh! very well, Mr. Stretcher. I accept your advertisement. Your apologies are unnecessary."

And Lord Pendlebury resumed his walk. His mind was occupied in considering with an earnestness and sagacity beyond his years the puzzling dilemma in which he saw his two friends to be placed. He was satisfied of Corcoran's good faith. The late Master in Chancery was a well-known man in Dublin society, lively, agreeable, amusing, not always either dignified or discreet, fond no less of conversation than of toddy, a favourite with men and women. Moreover, he was for his age an excellently preserved man. The late Mrs. Corcoran, now Mrs. Belldoran, at one time a handsome person, was Scotch, of good family, high bred, exceedingly particular in her bearing, manner, conversation, and associates.

They had married late in life. No children had blessed their union. Not understanding her husband's Irish nature, or his fondness for irony of speech and situation, and often disturbed by the flavour of his racy humour or the freedom of his manners, Mrs. Corcoran's confidence in her husband became seriously shaken. Suspicions were excited. Sharp words were exchanged. Mr. Corcoran, conscious of his own honesty, keenly resented his wife's reflections, and did what many a man foolishly does in such circumstances—he affected to become more extravagant than ever. An unusually hot matrimonial skirmish having taken place at Homburg, Mrs. Corcoran left her husband without notice, and, returning to London, placed herself in the hands of solicitors. Mulrooney and Cadge "got up" a case for her with exemplary readiness and disastrous success. A *cause célèbre* was tried at Westminster, for the pair had been married in England. A German waiter was produced, who swore to conduct on the part of the learned Master which satisfied the judge and shocked his friends. A divorce was decreed. Upon this Mr. Corcoran retired from the Mastership. He had a considerable fortune, and finding life in Dublin, notwithstanding the fact that many of his friends remained staunch, to be painfully changed for him, he resolved to take a tour in America. To be perfectly free from any embarrassing inquiries, he assumed the whimsical name of Fex.

Lord Pendlebury, as aide-de-camp to the Lord-Lieutenant, had seen a good deal both of Mr. Corcoran and his wife, and had been extremely shocked by the circumstances and results of the appeal to the Divorce Court. And now, when by a most extraordinary fatality they were brought together under conditions which seemed to be favourable to a reconciliation, here was a Canadian auditor-general, or some other official, expecting to meet Mrs. Belldoran, as his *fiancée*, at their port of destination. The young lord viewed his own position with some anxiety, and not without a sensation of amusement. Both parties had chosen to make him a confidant of their hostile griefs. He fancied that he detected on either side a tone of regret at the past, which might, were experienced tact only at hand, be nourished into some effort to retrieve its sorrowful and disastrous consequences. He was specially alive to the necessity of securing the aid of some woman of sense and spirit in the delicate task which circumstances had thrown upon him. Lady Peakman occurred to his mind, only to be discarded. He saw that Mrs. Belldoran would not suffer interference from any one of Lady Peakman's manners and temperament. There was only one other person even distantly available, namely, Mrs. McGowkie, a quaint, gentle, pleasant little Scotch wife, without a shadow of experience in the ways of the wicked world.

"Well," he said to himself, "there can be no harm in making them acquainted. The Scotchwoman's simplicity and genuineness may have some effect on the elder lady. And who knows? They may 'foregather,' as Mr. McGowkie would say."

So, before an hour was over, Lord Pendlebury had managed to bring the proud Mrs. Belldoran and the blushing little Mrs. McGowkie together. To the latter he had given no information. He left the two ladies to mature an acquaintance and exchange confidences if they pleased. At the same time the cunning young peer kept his friend upon the deck, engaged in a peripatetic conversation, during which he several times designedly took him past the place where the two ladies were sitting. Hence Corcoran and his former wife were obliged to exchange glances, and every time they did so their hearts were bleeding.

13 *

Mean time Mrs. McGowkie, being taken in hand by a superior tactician, had told her prouder countrywoman all about herself, and her early life, and her marriage, with unaffected, and not in the least vulgar or offensive, candour. There was a freshness about this young person which was soothing to Mrs. Belldoran's disquiet. The familiar native accent also fell with a gentle charm on the lady's heart.

"You know," said Mrs. McGowkie, prattling away, "it is so pleasant to feel you are really loved and respected by the man you marry—and so easy to agree with him. I never could imagine how two people who loved each other sufficiently to become man and wife could ever have a difference. He is the 'head of the wife,' as she is a 'crown unto her husband.'"

"Why, you silly little chit," said Mrs. Belldoran, looking down magnificently on this commonplace and inexperienced little sciolist. "Do you not know that very few people become man and wife because they love each other? There are much more ordinary and unsentimental reasons than that."

Mrs. McGowkie blushed.

" I know nothing about them, madam. If people choose to begin wrong, they must e'en end wrong."

"Ay, but again it is said that love matches generally end the *worst*. Affection is easily satiated. People get bored with each other's company, suspicious of each other's faith."

"Ay, that's people 'in the world,'" interrupted Mrs. McGowkie. "I've had little to do with the like of them. To their own master must they stand or fall. I am sure, my dear madam, you have no experience of that sort!"

Mrs. McGowkie's simple heart having been deeply pained by her companion's cynicism, she spoke this with some intensity of feeling and expression. In the earnestness of the moment she laid her hand, in its little brown kid glove, on the arm of her haughty companion, and gave it a gentle pressure. The lady looked embarrassed.

"Oh, believe me, lady," continued Mrs. McGowkie, adopting, in the warmth of her feeling, the language and accent of her home life, "Suld ye na ken it, as I trust in God ye doo, when twa hearts is in tune the ane wi th'ither, and baith takin their note from the Great Master in heaven, though noo and again earthly imperfections may waken a bit discord throo trouble or anger, His hand will sune set the chords aricht. He bindeth up the broken hearts; and surely He can harmonise the broken music of earnest an' loving souls."

"You know little of the world, my child," said the lady, bending over and kissing the soft blooming cheek, ere she rose and hastily retreated to her cabin. Mrs. McGowkie wiped away a tear-drop that was coursing down her face. It had not come from her own eye.

"Mebbe," she mused to herself, "I ha' done wrong. The puir leddy will dootless hae a sair heart of her ain. But it was a' true, and truth canna harm if it's kindly told."

CHAPTER XI.

THE DISCOVERY.

LADY PEAKMAN did not leave her berth. She was suffering from a violent headache. Sir Benjamin came and went. Araminta flitted in and out. The maids succeeded each other in their attendance. But her ladyship, in a state of prostration, would only open her eyes painfully and languidly. Every half hour the fine-toned bells rang out, first on the poop, then on the forward deck. As eight bells struck in the afternoon, that rancorous dinner gong again gave iron tongue to brazen discord. Although the knight came in and persuaded her to make an effort, she would not go to dinner. Nor would she eat. She sent away her maid to take an airing on deck. She simply wished to be alone.

Every one had gone to the saloon. Stewards could be heard passing to and fro along the corridors. Clattering dishes, chattering tongues, the clink of bottles and glasses at the bar, the noise of people talking on the other side of the saloon bulkhead, disturbed her painfully. She could not think. Her brain was throbbing with anxiety and terror.

Suddenly there was a knock at her door. Was it *that man* again ? No, he must be waiting on Sir Benjamin. Drawing her robe around her, she called out to the inquirer to come in. A head of a man, unknown to her, looking mysterious, was inserted through the half-open door. It gazed round. It vanished an instant. It came back immediately, with the body to which it belonged. To the body were attached two arms, and on the hand of one of the arms swung her ladyship's jewel-case.

" If you please, my lady," said the man, touching his hair in front, " may this be yours ? "

She hardly glanced at it. There was no necessity. She *felt* what it was. Her heart sank within
her. She knew that her name lay across the top of
it in proud letters of gold.

"Yes. Who are you? Where did you get it?"

"Mr. Crog, may it please your ladyship. Steerage
steward. This case was found, mum—my lady—
stowed away under the mattress of Sir Benjamin's
new valet, Mr. Stillwater."

"Gracious goodness!"

"Yes, my lady. Might you have given it to him
to take charge of, my lady?"

"Certainly not."

"Because," said Mr. Crog, "this morning early,
my lady, when eight bells rang — which is four
o'clock a.m., my lady—I was one of the stewards
that had to turn out, and I had occasion to
go and arrange some things, my lady, at the
main hatchway; and there, at that hour of the
morning, my lady, I see a figure cut across from

the port passage, here between the cabins, and run slap into Slovenly George — a sailor we calls by that name, my lady. Well, it was dark, and I shouldn't a known the individual, but the sailor speaks to him and he answers the sailor, and I recognises Mr. Stillwater's voice immediate. Says I to myself, my lady, 'What's this fellar a runnin' about the ship at this hour of the day for? And a carrying somethin' heavy in his hand, moreover?' Howsomever, I know that gentlemen on board is wanting their servants at all hours of the day *or* night, and so I says nothing at the time, but thinks I—'I'll watch your movements, Mr. Stillwater.' So I tips the wink to my friend Mr. Benbow, the steward of the first-class cabins amidships, larboard side, to look out sharp all round the cabin in making up the bed, and see if he could find anything; and he found this under the mattress, my lady. And, my lady, there's a description on board, and a reward offered for a man who has committed a murder *and* robbery ; and if it weren't that the walley had his hair as red as carrots, when it ought to ha' been dyed black, I would have him in irons ten minutes after dinner was over."

" How do you think he got it ? "

" He must ha' slipped in when you was asleep, my lady."

"Oh, dear ! " said her ladyship, giving a little scream. "Surely not ! How shocking ! A man in my room ! I should certainly have heard him. . . . Mr. Crog."

" My lady."

" Don't say anything about this. Now I come to think of it, Sir Benjamin, who is always very anxious about this valuable case, may have asked the man to take charge of it. No doubt that is the explanation. I will speak to Sir Benjamin. But I am none the less indebted to you. Here is a sovereign for you.

"Thank you, my lady," said Crog, who however

felt deeply disappointed that Mr. Stillwater was to be let off so easily.

"That will do now, Mr. Crog. You need not speak to Sir Benjamin about it. I shall see him directly after dinner, and if there is anything wrong I will send for you ; but I hope it is all right."

Mr. Crog vanished as mysteriously as he came. In returning to his quarters he slipped into Mr. Stillwater's cabin, to take an observation on his own account, being assured that at the moment the valet was in attendance on his master in the saloon.

" I don't half like the look of this cove," said Mr. Crog to himself. There was no special reason why Mr. Crog should have been seized with this pro- found suspicion of Mr. Stillwater, beyond the fact that Mr. Stillwater had proved too sharp for him. Mr. Crog's *amour propre* had been wounded by the quick rough way in which Mr. Stillwater had pulled him up on the subject of the division of plunder.

It is only human nature. If you take a man down even one peg, he will be ready to hold you a thief and a murderer on very slight evidence.

"Now," said Mr. Crog to himself, in continuance, "here's this cove's baggage. A large pockmantle, brown leather, wery seedy-looking, been a number, of woyages, leather cut and scratched all over. Ha! a stout hasp and a good lock too: don't want no intruders. No name thereon, leastways so far as I can see. Wot's this? '*Hôtel de l'Europe, Homburg,*' '*Kaiserhof, Köln.*' Where's that, I wonder? Then some place or other '*Monaco.*' '*Hôtel des Etoiles, Biarritz.*' Here's one torn off— lets see. 'r-n-l'— that's a railway station mark—'r-n-l.'" He took out the paper containing a description of the runaway. "Ha! 'Darnley' is the name of the place where the murder was committed. Well, this is rum, to say the least of it. Anything else? Hat-box—wot! A hat-box, Mr. Stillwater! You are a swell, for a walley out of place, you are!—Small trunk or case two feet long, with brass nails all over it. No other mark but 'Stillwater' in ink on the bottom. All locked up, tight as the specie-room.—Nothing else about? No, not even a pocket-handkercher. You're a dark un, Mr. Stillwater. 'Still waters run deep.' Ha, ha, ha!"

"Ha! ha! ha!" echoed a voice in the cabin, within a couple of feet of him. Mr. Crog turned sharply round, and his eyes encountered those of Mr. Stillwater, which at the moment were lit up with a dangerous sparkle. He promptly shut the door and locked it, putting the key in his pocket.

"What are you doing in here, Mr. Crog?" inquired the valet, in an angry tone. "You ain't the steward of this part of the ship, you know."

"Oh!" replied Mr. Crog, recovering a little from his surprise, "I wanted to see you, and I was waiting for you. I think I have some information about our much-needed friend."

"You do, do you?" replied Mr. Stillwater, searching Mr. Crog's eyes to their very depths, and not satisfied with the result.

"Yes. I believe I have him. There's a German has been lying among the men down there, where you were stowed away so snugly. He don't answer the description as to hair, et-settery, but you know it's easy to shave or dye, and if the rest suits, we hadn't need to stand on ceremony."

Mr. Stillwater looked at Mr. Crog again, with a quick, keen, penetrating inquiry. The steward, a powerful fellow, had recovered his assurance. The cabin in which they were standing was next to the mess-room of the engineers. Several of them could be distinctly heard talking on the other side.

"Now, guvnor," said Mr. Crog, thinking it advisable to remind him of this fact, "don't talk so loud, or those parties will overhear us. Come along with me, and we will take a peep at the cove I've spotted." Stillwater did not move.

"You've pocketed the key by mistake, Mr. Still-water. Open the door and come along."

Stillwater hesitated a moment. His face became dark and menacing, and his hand with an undecided motion sought, not the pocket where he had deposited the key, but his bosom.

"Bah!" said Mr. Crog, who was watching every movement, and he threw himself with all his force upon the man, and seized his hands. "You would try that on, would you?" He shouted, "Engineers there—help!"

A terrific struggle ensued within the narrow limits of the cabin. Stillwater, surprised for an instant by Mr. Crog's unexpected promptness, recovered himself with the resourceful readiness of a man accustomed to situations of danger, and well trained in all the arts of defence. He soon shook off Mr. Crog's grasp upon his arms, and, closing with him, threw him on his back upon the floor, with his head against the sofa, which ran along the ship's side of the cabin, a position which left the poor steward at his mercy. In the scuffle a revolver had dropped from the valet's breast, and fortunately for Mr. Crog at the moment, it was lying under him, to his great discomfort, so that his foe was unable to recover it. Mean time the steward's tongue had not been silent. Men were already knocking at the door. As Stillwater, kneeling on the breast of the prostrate Crog, was striving to get his powerful hands fairly fixed on his neck, an effort which Crog resisted as well as he could in his awkward position, two or three sturdy engineers, applying their shoulders to the slight panel which constituted the door, burst it in, with its fastenings, and they and the wreck came tumbling in together upon Mr. Stillwater and his intended victim.

The *soi-disant* valet displayed immense strength, and the blood which was afterwards found scattered on the white French paint showed how terrific was the struggle that ensued. But weight and numbers soon told, and in about five or six minutes Mr. Stillwater, with his hands artistically tied behind him in a way known only to sailors, his face bleeding and his clothes nearly torn off his back, was seated on the sofa, facing several panting and excited men, whose figures and dress gave proof of the prisoner's desperate force and energy.

Mr. Crog, more breathless and discomposed than the rest, was resting upon the edge of the lower berth, with one eye artificially closed and coloured, his side-face covered with blood from a scalp wound, and his general appearance, as a cabin steward, by no means as trim and taut as the ship's regulations required. He was intently studying, with the single eye that remained open, in which there seemed to play a malicious gleam, the face and aspect of the so-called Mr. Stillwater. And, indeed, that person's exertions had wrought in him

14 *

a remarkable transformation. His red hair had vanished. It was lying about the floor of the cabin in rough tags. He now showed black, ruffled, short-clipped hair, above a high, strongly-marked forehead. But his whiskers still bore their carroty colour, as it was now clear, produced by dyeing. His face showed marks of rough handling. It had assumed a pale bluish tinge. He replied to Mr. Crog's stare with a cynical grin, and muttered through his teeth—

"Ah! if I had only had another minute of loving caress on your neck, my friend, you and I might have died happy."

Mr. Crog was not inclined to reply. A sickly sensation came over him, and he lay down. Meantime the captain, who had been summoned, entered, and after Mr. Crog had been revived by some brandy, received an account of the extraordinary occurrence. Determined this time to act with caution, he sent a message to the so-called Mr. Fex, stating that a suspicious person had been discovered on board in the person of Sir Benjamin's valet, and begging that he would give him the benefit of his advice. The messenger found the ex-Master, Lord Pendlebury, and Sir Benjamin, together. They at once proceeded in company to the engineers' mess-room, to which the prisoner had been removed. As it was now dark, the swinging lamps over the table had been lit. The light fell on the expressive face of the captured man. Mr. Corcoran had no sooner glanced at it than he seized Lord Pendlebury's arm with a spasmodic grip, and said to him aside,—

" Pendlebury, that is the man, as sure as fate —the rascal from Homburg that gave evidence against me. He has shaved off his beard and dyed his whiskers; but I should know him if his face were skinned."

Lord Pendlebury instantly saw the importance of this discovery, but he whispered a caution to his friend for the present to say nothing about it.

"Now gentlemen," said the captain, "you shall first hear Mr. Crog's account of his acquaintance and dealings with this person, and then we can proceed to make other inquiries."

Mr. Crog, watching with his single eye the prisoner and his hearers alternately, told at great length, and in every particular, the story of his relations with the prisoner. When he stated that Mr. Stillwater's left eyebrow had borne on the first day out that mark which was designated in the description of the accused Darnley murderer, every one was struck with astonishment. And when he went on to speak of the engagement of the prisoner by Sir Benjamin Peakman, and to tell the story of his mysterious movements in the early morning, the knight became painfully interested.

"I thought," said Mr. Crog, "that maybe Sir Benjamin was requiring something during the night ——"

"Certainly not!" interrupted Sir Benjamin.

"He left me in my berth last night at ten o'clock, and I did not see him until eight this morning."

The knight's face grew pale with alarm as Mr. Crog, proceeding with his narrative, described the finding of her ladyship's jewel-case, and his own interview with Lady Peakman.

"I can settle Lady Peakman's difficulty in a moment," cried the knight. "I never said a word to this man about the case."

During Mr. Crog's narrative of his interview with Lady Peakman, the face of the so-called Stillwater had worn a sardonic smile. At the exclamation of the knight, he opened his lips.

"Lady Peakman gave me the case herself," he said, quietly.

The four gentlemen looked at each other.

"Shut up, you rascal," cried the captain. "You are a liar."

"Well, if you bring Lady Peakman here, I will

soon get her to own to it," said the fellow, with a malicious grin.

"Do not take Lady Peakman's name into your mouth, sir!" said the knight, smiling in his most enraged manner. "Your story only confirms our impression that you are a dangerous fellow."

"Her name has been very often in my mouth," said Mr. Stillwater, "and will be again, Sir Benjamin, before I have done with you."

"I shall have you gagged, if you don't keep your mouth shut," said the captain. "Go on Crog."

Mr. Crog finished his recital with an account of the struggle in the cabin, pointing out the disclosures which had resulted from it in the extraordinary change wrought upon Mr. Stillwater's personal appearance.

"Has he any luggage?" asked Mr. Corcoran.

Crog answered in the affirmative.

"Then, captain, I should have it searched."

The prisoner's face grew deadly pale.

"Mr. Turbot," said the captain to the first officer, "remove all the baggage into the mail-room, and examine it carefully in the presence of the mail-officer. Make out a list of everything found."

"Now," said Mr. Corcoran, looking again sharply at the prisoner, "look at me, sir. Have you ever seen me before?"

The man examined him an instant with a cool scrutiny, and a flash of recognition passed swiftly over his features, followed by a smile, which made them more ghastly than ever.

"O yaus! Corcorran—and Cor-corran," said the man, adopting a foreign accent. "I remember well ze Meinheer und Frau at ze Hotel of ze Ambassadors at Homburg—eh?"

"I thought so," said Mr. Corcoran. "And you gave evidence at Westminster?"

"Yes."

"Pendlebury," said the ex-Master, "will you see if you can get a certain lady to step down here?"

As Lord Pendlebury left the cabin, the *ci-devant* Mr. Fex turned to the captain and asked him to have the room cleared of all except the three gentlemen. By the time this had been done, and a guard had been established at the door, the peer returned. Leaning on his arm, in a highly excited state, was Mrs. Belldoran.

As she entered, the gentlemen rose. Mr. Corcoran was at the upper end of the table, about ten feet from the door. Their eyes met. They bowed to each other. The captain and Sir Benjamin watched the scene with curiosity and surprise.

"Madam," said Mr. Corcoran, politely, "a very extraordinary thing has happened, which has led me to put you to the pain and trouble of this interview. Our common friend, Lord Pendlebury, agrees with me that it is desirable you should be present."

Lord Pendlebury bowed.

" Do you know this man ? " said Mr. Corcoran, pointing gravely to Mr. Stillwater.

Mrs. Belldoran looked earnestly at the prisoner, and coloured violently. She put her hand on her heart, and staggered to a seat. Lord Pendlebury hastened to her, but she recovered with a few whiffs from the scent-bottle.

" I scarcely recognise him," she said, "for I only saw the person twice in my life, to my knowledge. He is much altered. But he is the man who — who——"

" Precisely," interrupted Mr. Corcoran, gently, " who committed perjury in the case of Corcoran *v.* Corcoran."

" Perjury ! " exclaimed Mrs. Belldoran.

" Yes. *Perjury*, madam. What do *you* say, sir ? "

" A man is not bound to criminate himself," replied the prisoner, coolly. " You are a lawyer, sir, and know that as well as I do."

In speaking these words, this extraordinary individual appeared to assume a new character. His manner became dignified, and his tone was that of a cultivated gentleman.

" True, Mr. What's-your-name. But you are now in a serious position. And it was on your evidence chiefly that the Judge-Ordinary relied — that this lady was deceived — that a great and terrible calamity has come upon two innocent people."

"Pooh!" said the man, the blackguard coming out of him again. " All that is a matter of sentiment. People that will go into the Divorce Court are not much concerned about either dignity or decency, innocence or guilt. I was paid to help you both out of a scrape," he said, glancing with an impudent smile at Mrs. Belldoran, "and I was very happy to be of service to you."

"You bad man!" cried the lady, " Do you mean to say you perjured yourself? What induced you to commit such a wickedness ? "

"You did, madam, through your solicitors, or rather through the agents they employed to get up the evidence. It was very easy for one so well used to the world and its ways as I am to imagine on your behalf those peccadilloes which it was desired to bring home to your husband."

Mrs. Belldoran wrung her hands and raised her eyes to the ceiling. Lord Pendlebury, with exquisite tact, gave her his hand, and led her from the cabin.

"You admit, then," said Mr. Corcoran, "that the evidence you gave before the Ordinary in the suit of Corcoran v. Corcoran was false?"

"If it will give you any satisfaction for me to admit it," replied the man. "Yes. Though, for my part," he added, shrugging his shoulders, "I don't understand your wishing to know it. You were set at liberty by my testimony from a troublesome connection. I should scarcely have thought, from my own experience, that you would have been anxious to put on the noose again."

" Happily my motives, feelings, and sentiments are not submitted for your opinion," replied Mr. Corcoran, with severity. " Gentlemen, I may rely on you to carry in your minds the important statement we have heard. By some singular and blessed Providence I appear to have been brought on board this vessel, to find at once the means of clearing myself from a cloud which was resting on my life, and of convincing one for whom I had a deep and sincere affection that she has been the victim of a villainous perjury."

Lord Pendlebury here returned, and was immediately followed by the first officer. The latter carried in his hand a packet of papers. They had been found concealed in the false bottom of the prisoner's portmanteau. Among them were several bonds and other documents, shown by the endorsements to belong to the " Darnley Branch of the

National Provincial Bank." More important still, a small dagger, wrapped in a handkerchief covered with blood, had been found hidden in the casing of the hat-box. The manager of the Darnley Branch Bank, as every one knew from the newspapers, had, when working late one night in the office of the bank—the upper portion of which was used as his dwelling-house—been stabbed to the heart by a single blow, delivered over his right shoulder by an expert and powerful assassin. So noiselessly and quickly had the crime been committed, that the wife and servants of the victim, who were sleeping upstairs, knew nothing of it until, waking towards morning, the lady descended, to find her husband cold and dead, and the safe of the bank rifled.

When these evidences were adduced, Mr. Stillwater's face became a ghastly green. His confidence vanished; his head drooped; he seemed to be completely overpowered. The captain ordered that he should be heavily ironed and confined in the carpenter's room, which abutted on the space surrounding the main hatchway on the spar-deck. Two armed sailors patrolled around this marine prison.

CHAPTER XII.

THE RESURRECTION OF HOPE.

LADY PEAKMAN'S first impulse, when Sir Benjamin related to her with graphic *verve* and particularity the story of the terrible scene in which his valet had been the ignoble hero, and of the still more terrible discovery that had ensued upon it, was to faint away. And she yielded to the impulse. Sir Benjamin naturally, and the doctor scientifically, attributed the syncope to the shock given by a horrible surprise to an enfeebled system. On her recovery, all that she demanded was quiet. In the quiet she wept and prayed. She felt certain that this ruffian, who knew so much, would now, out of mere malice, if from no other motive, let out the secret of her early life — of his relations to her.

15

It was true that she had honestly believed him to be dead. Moreover, it was true that, since he had left her, she had been a very changed woman. But as she lay there, swiftly reviewing all her life since then, she recalled to herself how much of that better existence had been given to mere selfishness and pride: to how many she—a reclaimed sinner—had been a harsh and unrelenting critic, nay, frequently a cruel censor; and how often she had pursued the aims of her paltry ambition to be something in society, by means which her awakened conscience now recalled with disgust and sorrow.

It is in those hours, when all our plans seem to be failing, and disaster or humiliation threaten to overwhelm us, that we realise with the most startling clearness the exact value or worthlessness of our most cherished aims, our dearest triumphs. Lady Peakman saw before her only mortification, exposure, her husband's anger and hatred—for she knew well how he would be affected by the inevitable discovery — and her daughter's lifelong shame.

Nevertheless, out of the depths her poor heart, feebly reaching forth in the darkness for something to lay hold of, cried out in anguish to the unseen and eternal Helper.

But the interest excited in the vessel by the extraordinary events of the afternoon soon yielded to the livelier sensations caused by a brisk and growing gale from the north-east, which towards ten o'clock that evening created among the passengers familiar and irrepressible horrors. Once more the hatches were battened down, the deadlights were screwed on, and the roar without was almost deafened by the tumult within. There was a general collapse. The gale increased steadily during the night, and by Wednesday morning the ship was scudding before it at the rate of fourteen knots an hour. Everything gave way to the overpowering influences. What are sentiment, or sor-

row, or fear, or mortification, or good will, when
man or woman has no stomach for anything ? In
such circumstances you lie indifferent to the loss of
your wife, and might even view without a pang the
drowning of your wife's mother. Mr. Corcoran,
Mrs. Belldoran, Lord Pendlebury, Lady Peakman,
Sir Benjamin, Mrs. McGowkie, Miss Araminta, and
many another, might on that morning be said to be
tossing about with all their ordinary purposes and
wishes in a state of suspended animation. During
those dreary hours some of them may have wished
that they could die.

It is certain that Lady Peakman would have
done so if she could. It was the only thought that
crossed again and again her fevered brain. She
wished a higher power would decree that her
misery should end. At length she fell into an
uneasy slumber—a doze, wherein the noise of the
howling storm and the loud anguish of the creak-
ing ship were mixed up with the grim shadows

of sorrow and despair which hovered around her excited brow.

How long she lay in this frightful doze she knew not. But at length she started up with a shriek. Her cabin door had opened—she thought a man was standing between her and the light — she thought his hand was stretched out, was already clutching her throat. — There *was* a man. His hand was unloosing the knitted hood she wore tied round her face and neck. She looked again. It was her husband. A cheerful morning sun was shining through the round-eyed port. The time was past eight o'clock.

"Oh!" she cried, shudderingly, as she caught sight of his face, which looked pale and alarmed. "I thought it was——" She stopped, and clasped her hands together.

"The thief, I suppose you were going to say? No, I thought you were ill. You were struggling and mumbling in your sleep, and I was afraid you were going to have a fit, so I was undoing your hood. How do you feel now?"

She fell back.

"Oh," she said, "it was a nightmare. How came you here so early?"

"I have been called up. A terrible thing has happened, and I desired that you should learn it at once, and from myself, lest you should be told of it suddenly by the women. It relates to that wretched creature who was called Stillwater."

She closed her eyes.

"It is all coming," she said to herself, and setting her teeth together, braced herself as bravely as she could for what she felt certain was to follow.

"Do you remember," the knight went on, quietly, "that when you first saw him you showed a great aversion to him? I saw your glance, and evidently his aspect was repulsive to you, partly no doubt because of the villainous red hair he had assumed for a disguise. I can assure you he looked much better without it. Indeed, for a Jewish-faced rascal, he was not such a bad-looking fellow. Well, yesterday he was shut up in the carpenter's cabin, heavily ironed. He could, however, move his hands about, and lift them. Two men were placed outside, to guard him. They looked in on him last night at about twelve. You know how rough it was. A mattress had been arranged for him on the floor. He seemed to be lying on the mattress quietly enough. This morning at six the watch entered and found him dead."

"DEAD!" cried Lady Peakman, sitting up in her berth, and looking at the knight in a way that startled him. " Dead, did you say?"

" Yes. He managed during the night to get hold of a sharp bradawl or auger, and with that he opened veins in both arms. The doctor says the man must have understood the business perfectly. The mattress was found deluged in blood, and he lay there quite cold. It is a horrible thing."

" Horrible ! " echoed Lady Peakman, lying down
again and closing her eyes.

Who could imagine what a torrent of conflicting
emotions then surged through her mind! The man
was dead whom she had believed to be dead before.
Twice dead for her, each time, alas, most welcomely.
This man, whom she had once loved, and yet
whose resurrection had shaken her with a horror
which was the most awful experience of her life.
Dead ? Alas, poor wretch ! Gone to his account
wicked and unrepentant. Dead ? Ay, what a
relief ! He can no longer threaten her. Her secret
is buried with him.

She was unconscious of Sir Benjamin's presence,
waiting for her eyes to open, and her lips to speak.
He addressed her. She turned her face and looked
at his with a strange look he could not understand.
She took his hand and clasped it nervously,
warmly. Tears ran down her face.

" This terrible business has exhausted you,"

he said. "There now, lie down and be quiet awhile."

And he went out, leaving her to her own thoughts.

She knew not what to think of this strange, unlooked-for deliverance. It was scarcely possible to believe in it. Was it even right to accept it? So deeply, so truly had she realised all the terrors of exposure, that now, to be certain that the danger was removed, that only she and God held the secret, that her husband's and her daughter's honour were safe, seemed incredible, unreal. Yet the sense of relief gradually won its way over her mental and physical frame. And slowly it brought with it a blessed humbling influence. Turning to her Bible, she cast her eye over psalm after psalm, and words which humanity has ever found to be the fittest to express the deepest and most powerful emotions of the soul, welled up like a spring out of the experiences of past ages, as fresh, as reviving, as if they had been written for her to-day.

" Out of the depths have I cried unto thee, O Lord. Lord, hear my voice, and the voice of my supplication. If thou, Lord, shouldest mark iniquity, O Lord, who shall stand ? But there is forgiveness with thee, that thou mayest be feared. . . . My soul waiteth for the Lord, more than they that watch for the morning. I say, more than they that watch for the morning."

If we say that out of this dreadful experience this woman by-and-by came forth altered, softened, chastened, bettered, who shall scorn it ? The old life passed away. It died, with all its evil influences—and was buried. It had only slumbered when *he*—the Mephistopheles of its worst period —had awhile disappeared. There had been no real repentance. But now that he was gone who had come back in circumstances so horrible, now that the menace of a fearful retribution had de-

parted from her, now that she could safely bury
the past with him, she felt that a gentler spirit
came in and took possession of her heart, she
felt as if a humbling, but a holy influence had
breathed upon her life. It was a shuddering dread
to turn and gaze again upon that morose departing
cloud carrying away with it the mist and darkness
of a hard experience. But how much brighter
shone the sun whose beams now cheered her way.

And it was clear that all this must for ever
be locked in her own breast. The secret of her
changed manners, pursuits, hopes, could not be
revealed. To tell it to Sir Benjamin, would be to
inflict a needless, and perhaps a remediless, pain.
For her innocent daughter's sake nothing must
be risked. There was no human being with whom
this burden should be shared. Perhaps it might
be left where the pilgrim in the allegory left it;
but if not, it must be carried bravely by her—alone.

God is ever more pitiful than man. He had

closed up and sealed over for this poor, proud, erring
woman, such a past as a malignant society would
have rejoiced to peer into, to uncover, to dissect,
to set up in the light of day as a most delightful
scandal. Could we, ever needing pity, only be as
compassionate as He who requires it not! Could
we, men and women, only imitate the Divine
benevolence, and charitably veil for our brethren
and sisters their dead disastrous past, in order to
render more fruitful of hope the redeeming future!
Could our Christmas time, our Christmas church-
goings, our Christmas greetings, our Christmas
pleasures, only bring near to us the spirit of the
Christmas Childling, who in His manhood looking
sadly upon discovered sin, reproved its malignant
and hypocritical censors, while to the trembling
sinner He gently said: *"Neither do I condemn
thee. Go in peace, and sin no more!"*

CHAPTER XIII.

THE RECONCILIATION.

THERE were many signs on board the *Kams-chatkan* that its mariners were soon expecting to approach the land. The passengers now becoming accustomed to the motion of the ship, and tempted by the finer weather, gladly watched the sailors, under the direction of the quartermasters, busily overhauling the tackling and covering of the boats, or here and there, where there were marks of weather, putting on injured bulwarks a patch of paint; or, in that deliberate but skilful way in which sailors do these odd jobs, splicing, and reeving, and sewing, and tarring stays, braces, ropes, rigging, netting, or tarpaulins which had been injured by the weather. The voyage had

been an unexpectedly rapid one, and there was
every hope of reaching Portland by Sunday afternoon, the 23rd of December.

On Friday, with a brisk breeze from the east, and
a bright sun sparkling on the blue rolling waves
with their crowns of snowy spray, it was a pleasure
to pace the deck and gossip and watch the sailors
at work, or the crowds of steerage passengers
lounging about the warm quarters of the smoke
funnels with their iron casings.

Lady Peakman was able to come up on deck—
pale, weak, an altered woman. Araminta, happily
unconscious of her mother's thoughts, was in a
mood as bright and sparkling as the little wavelets
that danced off the sharp bow of the glancing
vessel. Wrapt in an ermine cloak, and with a
scarlet feather in a little deer-stalking hat, she
looked very saucy and dazzling. So thought Lord
Pendlebury when he emerged from the smoking-
room. where he had been amusing himself over his

pipe with the conversation of Mr. Weiss and the
Ottawa editor, whose failure to discover the fugitive
Kane left him at the mercy of the cunning and
stolid German. The editor, however, was consoling himself with the thought that he only of
"all the journalists in creation" was at present
acquainted with the romantic and thrilling events
which had occurred on board the *Kamschatkan*,
and which would render her outward voyage one
of the most memorable on record. He was
already calculating how many dollars he would
get out of the "New York Flasher" and other
transatlantic journals for a highly-spiced and sen-
sational account which he was preparing to send
on speculation by telegraph from Portland. He
was therefore not in so bad a humour as his dearest
friends would have desired.

The decease of the man Kane, *alias* Stillwater,
alias Moreno, &c., had been made the subject of a
grave consultation in the captain's chart-room. Lord

Pendlebury, Mr. Corcoran, Sir Benjamin Peakman, and Mr. Carpmael had been called in to assist the skipper with their advice. It was decided that the body should be thrown overboard after the doctor had made a careful examination and written an accurate description of the deceased. Mr. Carpmael was of opinion that the evidences of identity were sufficient without producing the remains, which, in any case, would have been of no use unless sent to England. Thus the last faint possibility that the dead man might be identified as the *quondam* Count Stracchino was removed. Lord Pendlebury, as an English justice of the peace, and Mr. Carpmael, as a commissioner to take oaths for Canada, then took written depositions of all the persons who had any evidence to offer concerning the deceased, and these were placed in the captain's hands. This solemn business over, every one was glad to dismiss from his mind the horrid episode.

*　　　*　　　*　　　*

Another meeting had taken place. When Mrs. Belldoran left the room where the culprit was under examination, she was stunned by the revelation he had made. Idle and baseless as her suspicions were now proved to have been, she had honestly believed in them. The bitterness of the thought that he had wronged her had hardened her heart against Corcoran, and she came on board the *Kamschatkan* with a clear conscience and a real satisfaction that she was about to shake off the memory of her former marriage, and to join her lot with one whom she esteemed to be in every way more worthy of her affections than the discarded Master in Chancery. But events had touched her heart. It was impossible to see him again, to know that he was miserable, to learn that he asserted his innocence, without a painful convulsion of heart. Moreover, the words of Mistress McGowkie, few and simple as they were, produced a strong effect. Mrs. Belldoran's resentment was softened.

But her embarrassment was keen, almost agonising. She was legally freed from this man whom she still conceived to have injured her, and she was under an engagement to another to whom her affections had been honourably pledged. Yet now the earlier love, and the memories of a happier past, and the promptings of a noble forgiveness, which Mrs. McGowkie had so inartificially but powerfully suggested, all wrought upon the mind and heart of the *divorcée*. In this state of her feelings, there came the confession of the criminal. With a woman's quick deduction she accepted the man's statement as true without a question. She had been deceived. Instead of being wronged, she was the wronging one. She forgot all the unhappy circumstances which had contributed gradually to bring her to the conviction of her husband's unfaithfulness. As her heart melted, sorrow settled upon it. She was without a friend to share and to sympathise with her difficulty.

In this extremity the proud lady turned to the little Scotchwoman. Her maid was sent off with peremptory orders to produce Mrs. McGowkie in the purser's cabin at once. Mrs. McGowkie came. In the moist and melting interview which ensued, there was perhaps a good deal said that was soft, and not a little that was incoherent and absurd; but the feeling in both hearts was genuine, and Mrs. McGowkie's quaint religion and unaffected purity and artlessness of character helped in no small degree to dissolve the more worldly ideas and prejudices of the elder lady.

"Of course ye'll be for seeing him," said Mrs. McGowkie—it was on this very Friday morning —"and you will just talk it all over together; and doubtless, by the blessing of God, now that its a' cleared up, ye'll be able to see eye to eye again —and may God bless ye both, my dear lady."

And squeezing Mrs. Belldoran's hand affectionately, while tears were bathing both their faces, the

16 *

little Scotchwoman turned to the glass, as she wiped her eyes, and glanced into it, to see whether she was fit to present herself to company. Then she stepped out of the cabin into the clear sunny daylight.

Lord Pendlebury was talking to Araminta, beside whom reclined her ladyship. Mrs. McGowkie tripped along the deck, hoping that the peer would see her and join her, for she shrank from coming into contact with haughty Lady Peakman. Lord Pendlebury, however, was too absorbed in Miss Araminta's lively and naïve conversation to notice any one else, so that at length Mrs. McGowkie was obliged to put a bold face on it, and approach the group. The exciting interview through which she had passed had brightened her colour, a wee tell-tale tear still glistened on one eyelash, and her nervousness showed itself in her quick and hesitating manner. Lady Peakman no sooner saw her than she raised herself from her recumbent posture, and held out her hand frankly and kindly. There was a painfu' pallor on her face.

" How do you do, Mrs. McGowkie? I am happy to see that you don't appear to have suffered much by the voyage."

Mrs. McGowkie was surprised by the graciousness of this reception, and hardly knew how to acknowledge it. She said, however, the first thing her heart dictated, which happened to be the right thing, and her sweet Scotch accent and silvery tremulous voice sounded very soothing to the ears of the weary and sorrowful dame. Araminta was pleased to emulate her mamma and to be very gracious, the more that Lord Pendlebury at length rose and addressed Mrs. McGowkie with emphatic kindness and deference. She told him at length that she wished to speak to him. Giving her his arm, they walked away. This time no ill-natured remark fell from her ladyship, though Araminta looked a little disturbed.

In a few minutes the peer had been made acquainted with the state of affairs.

"You had best just ask the gentleman to walk straight into the cabin next his own, and talk to her himself," said Mrs. McGowkie, with the singular decisiveness that is natural to all her countrymen and countrywomen. "They must e'en settle it together, ye see, for there's no one else can do it for them."

Lord Pendlebury looked with such a gleam of quizzical admiration into the pretty blue eyes opposite to him, that the good little lady blushed scarlet, though a pleasant smile played about her lips. He left her, and hastened to the captain's cabin, where he found Corcoran in great distress. He was listening to weeping in the neighbouring room, and tears stood in his own eyes.

"Pendlebury," he said, when he saw his friend, "this cannot last. I must see *her*," pointing with his finger towards the purser's cabin. "She is not happy, and I am sure that I am in an intolerable state."

The peer took his hand.

"My dear Corcoran," he said, "I came to tell you to go in and speak to her frankly and confidently—to assure you that you may safely do so. She is waiting—she will be glad to see you. A little bird has told me."

"You don't say so?" said Corcoran, with native impulsiveness, and without another word he darted out of the captain's cabin and into the next. Lord Pendlebury, anxious to avoid overhearing any portion of the interview, stepped quickly out of the room and shut the door. We shall imitate his delicacy. * * * * *

A half-hour passed—an hour. The young peer, filled with anxiety which he could not suppress, and feeling unable to resume the bantering conversation with Miss Araminta, paced the deck from amidships to the poop and back again, watching

the door of the purser's cabin. The lunch bell
had rung, but there was no sign. The deck became clear of passengers. Still Lord Pendlebury
walked up and down. At length the purser's door
opened. Corcoran emerged. He glanced round
quickly, and perceiving Pendlebury, beckoned to
him, and rushed into the captain's cabin.

"Thank God! my dear fellow!" cried the Irishman, squeezing the young lord's hand with great
warmth. "It's all settled! She's my own once
more. I'll never forget you for this, my dear
friend. She's as gentle as a child. All the old
love come back again. To think we must go back
to the altar, to be man and wife once more! I'll
be a Roman Catholic after this—they are right—
the law of divorce is most wicked and unnatural!
Take my advice, my friend. Never have a divorce
under any circumstances."

Lord Pendlebury restrained his amusement at
the whimsical mixture of humour and good feeling

displayed by the worthy ex-Master. He congratulated him heartily on the reconciliation.

"Your Christmas will be a merry one, at all events," he said, cheerily.

" Faith, it will be merrier than *his*," he said, pointing in the direction of the land. " It's hard—eh?—robbing a poor fellow of an expected wife at this time of year, when he was looking out for her as a Christmas-box. But the difficulty is only beginning. What is to be done? Maybe he's an irascible customer, and he might shoot me, or perhaps the barbarous laws of this new country may deny me the right to marry my own wife again. Any way, there will be a scene. It is precious unpleasant."

" Let me think of a way out of that difficulty. Meanwhile, Corcoran, come with me, and let me introduce you to the dear little lady to whom you are most indebted for this happy re-arrangement. Forgive the word, but what else can I call it?"

CHAPTER XIV.

A RUNAWAY MATCH.

DELAYED by a fog, it was early on Monday
morning, the eleventh day out, when the
Kamschatkan, steaming through the great opening of Casco bay, approached the harbour of
Portland. On board all was excitement and
preparation. Passengers, officers, seamen, stewards,
and baggage, were mixing themselves up in a con-
glomerate that promised to be insoluble. Above
the stirring scene, on the bridge, the pilot, who had
been picked up thirty miles away, coolly chatted
with the captain as they watched the points of the
lapping headlands opening up one after the other.
Joyous seemed the morning sun and enlivening the
brisk keen wind that came off the snow-spread

country, on which rested so many curious eyes.
The Canadian and American passengers were
anxiously calculating their chances of reaching
home in time for the celebration of Christmas
—a day and an idea which carries all round the
great world an unbroken circle of festivity ; and
their brightened fancy looked forward to affec-
tionate greetings and pleasures doubled by glad
reunion. But to the majority it was a chill and
wondering look-out. What Christmas cheer was
there for them in that vast ice-sprent land, among
a strange people and in circumstances so new and
so painful? Little Miss Beckwith, gazing earnestly
at the approaching shore as she stood alone by the
wheelhouse, drew her thin cloak closer round her
spare figure, and shuddered not so much at the
cold as with sorrowful apprehension. Some one,
however, had been looking at the thin blue face,
and came up abruptly, but with a kindly gentleness in his voice. It was Sandy McGowkie. His

countenance was a picture of efflorescent comfort
and good health.

"Eh! Miss Beckwith," he cried. "This will be
a cold look-out for ye! But it's not so cold when
you get to it, as it looks from here, and feels, too.
Ye seem to be half frozen. I'll warrant ye've
never thought of getting yourself any warm winter
clothing, now!"

"O yes, I am quite warm enough, thank you,
Mr. McGowkie," cried the little woman, a faint
dash of blood flushing the skin for a moment, but
never changing the blue of the brave lips which
she pressed closely together to stop the tremor, lest
it should belie her words.

"Ay, but not enough," persisted Sandy. "Ye're
for Montreal, now, are ye not?"

"Yes," she said.

"Ah! well now, Mistress McGowkie was just
saying that you'd be unco' lonely and sad to-
morrow, for a stranger in a strange land, and we'll

be lonely too. Ye'll just please go on with us, and eat a Christmas dinner at St. Lawrence Hall, for I'm thinking we shall not get all the way home to Toronto in time. Come away, now, and get a big shawl, to keep ye warm. It's a new one, and they'll pass it more readily at the customs if it's on your back, and we shall be greatly obliged to ye."

Following Mr. McGowkie to the cabin he occupied jointly with his wife, the governess was soon wrapped up cosily in a huge, soft, lambswool shawl, and the touch of a generous sympathy sent a glow through her shivering heart.

" Eh ! " cried McGowkie, " but where is my wifie, now ? Ay ! ay ! she'll be away with that young lord, looking after they doitering *divorsees*, as she calls them. Hout ! What a matter these quarrelling mates make o' life ! Ye'll just come with me then and indicate your luggage, and I'll see that it goes with ours ; and, mind ye, if ye please, ye'll be our guest so long as we are together, and you'll not mention a syllable about the expenses, or I'll cast ye off, bag and baggage."

Mrs. McGowkie was indeed engaged in the purser's cabin. To avoid a scene on the boat or on the pier, which would have been inevitable had the expectant bridegroom recognised the lady, it had been decided at a council held in the captain's cabin that Mrs. Belldoran and Mr. Corcoran must be smuggled ashore in disguise, and get away from Portland as soon as possible. How this was to be accomplished, without attracting the attention of the general company, and in the teeth of the fact that the lady's name and that of her maid were on the purser's list, and would at once be seen by the inquiring official, as soon as he came on board, was a problem which had puzzled Lord Pendlebury's ingenuity, and greatly perplexed the simple soul of Mistress McGowkie. She had the gravest doubts about lending her assistance to a scheme of decep-tion which was, in her eyes, worse even than play-acting, because it was so real. Indeed, she urged Mr. Corcoran to brave the difficulty, and just "meet the poor man and tell him the truth." But the ex-Master knew himself too well to agree to this.

"It will never do, my dear lady," he said. "Do you think a man gives up a woman with a thousand a year and good connections, without a struggle? He would wish to see her, and then he would reproach her, and then he would threaten her, and then, maybe, he would run clean off with her; and in this blessed democratic country, for all I know, law and public opinion would go with him. And then, where would I be?"

The ex-Master put this question with such melancholy earnestness, that the peer, who was listening to the conversation, laughed aloud, and even Mrs. McGowkie could not repress her smiles.

So the little Scotchwoman, considering that it was a right thing to help "to bind up broken hearts," yielded to her good nature, and was aiding and abetting in an elaborate plan which had been devised to enable the separated couple to execute a runaway match.

Lord Pendlebury's neighbour at the dinner table was a Boston clergyman, and he had informed the peer that a marriage could be legally performed in the United States between two persons of full age before any minister, and without a license. It was therefore arranged that the pair should accompany him to Boston by the first train, which would leave upon the arrival of the steamer, and that the ceremony should be performed by him on Christmas morning.

" A good day for a good deed," said Mr. Corcoran.

The unhappy Mr. Freemantle, who had turned out of the St. Louis House as soon as the vessel had been signalled, was now walking up and down on the slippery pier in a state of preternatural excitement, as the *Kamschatkan*, moving majestically through the smooth deep water of the magnificent harbour, drew up alongside. His eye eagerly scanned the faces which thronged the port bulwarks in a long line from stem to stern. But he looked in vain. The wished-for face of the *fiancée* was wanting. Again and again he searched the crowd on the stern deck, always to be disappointed. Slowly the huge ship moved. Lines were thrown into boats and towed ashore ; cables were attached to the big posts on the pier ; the donkey engine worked away with its short, quick, rub-a-dub strokes, and gradually, deliberately, with exasperating slowness, the floating mass came nearer and nearer to the pier. But no Mrs Belldoran was to be seen at the bulwarks with a waving handkerchief and a smiling welcome. Lord Pendlebury, coolly chatting for the moment with Araminta, but really in a state of the deepest anxiety, watched the crowd of persons collected on the pier, to see if he could discover the auditor-

17

general, whose person had been described to him by Mrs. Belldoran. At this moment the purser appeared at the bulwarks and threw a book to a clerk of the shipping firm, who was waiting on the pier. The purser was not in the secret. A gentleman standing near the clerk said to him quickly—

"Is that the purser?"

"Yes, sir."

"Purser!" he shouted. "Is there a Mrs. Belldoran on board?"

"Yes," answered the officer. "Purser's cabin."

Lord Pendlebury started. There, no doubt, was Mr. Freemantle, and he would be aboard in five minutes. Without a word of apology to Miss Peakman the peer darted off, and pushed his way through the crowd that occupied the fore-deck. There he found a man dressed in the uniform of one of the ship's stewards, with a low cap on, prominently peaked. To his arm was clinging a person dressed in a somewhat seedy costume, but whose large and showy figure very ill supported the character she had assumed of a lady's-maid. A thick blue veil covered her face.

"He is there!" cried Lord Pendlebury, in a whisper. He pointed out to the supposed steward the unconscious Cœlebs, who, wrapped in a warm coat of Astrachan fur, seemed to be anxious to leap upon the vessel. Corcoran felt the hand on his arm clutch it convulsively and tremble.

The peer joined Nick Donovan, Mr. Corcoran's servant, who was waiting at the steerage gangway, ready to be the first to rush ashore and secure a hack to convey the fugitives to the Boston dépôt.

"There is the gentleman, Nick, in the big black fur coat."

"Stand back there!" cried a voice. The vessel had touched the pier. A number of men seized upon a broad gangway. The ropes were already

17 *

aboard, and half-a-dozen sailors dragged it up to the space that had been opened in the bulwarks. The steerage gangway was up first. Regardless of cries and curses, the man in the fur coat rushed breathless up the wooden bridge, brushing past the peer and the servant.

"Where is the purser's cabin?" he shouted.

"Oh!" screamed Mrs. Belldoran. Corcoran placed his hand over her mouth.

"Silence, my dear—for the love of heaven and me!" he whispered. But the inquirer had been too excited to notice the exclamation of the steerage passenger. He pushed forward. At the same time Lord Pendlebury and Nick Donovan were running along the pier and through the yard of the Grand Trunk Railway, to the outer area where sleighs were in waiting. Nick held in his hands two travelling-bags and a bundle of rugs. A sleigh and pair were easily obtained. The peer hastened back, to find the fugitives, in their excitement, losing themselves in the mazes of the great goods-station. They reached the sleigh, and rapidly ensconced themselves in the buffalo robes.

"You have no time to lose," said Lord Pendlebury. "A merry Christmas to you, Corcoran, and to you, *Mrs. Corcoran,*—I may say I hope?"

"God bless you, my dear Pendlebury!" cried the ex-Master. "May ye never elope yourself in less happy circumstances. I suppose the parson will turn up in good time for the train? Tell our—our *friend* we are grieved that necessity obliges us to play him such a scurvy trick; and you might perhaps add that he has lost nothing by it!—Eh, Pearl?—A merry Christmas to you, my dear fellow!"

Mrs. Belldoran's grasp was no less warm and cordial. She could scarcely speak. Tears were in her eyes.

"My dear boy," she said, "you have played the part of an old and experienced friend. In restoring our peace, may you add to your own. A thousand thousand blessings on you!"

As the young peer turned away, touched by the feeling she had shown, he overheard Corcoran addressing his servant.

"Nick!"

"Yes, sir!"

"Go aboard now, and look after the things of myself and my lady, and get them through the customs in good order. And see here now, closer. Don't ye be making up to my lady's maid, and running away with her. It's a disreputable way of doing things. If you manage this all right, I'll settle something handsome on you for life. Good-bye now. You will follow by the next train to Boston, and look us up at the Commonwealth Hotel."

Lord Pendlebury hastened back to the ship, where by this time the injured Mr. Freemantle was creating a lively scene. When he rushed off to the purser's cabin, the eager bridegroom found its door closed and locked. He knocked gently on the panel. No answer. More loudly. No reply. Still louder.

"Who's there?" cried a voice from the inside of the cabin.

"'Tis she!" said Freemantle. "I am here, my love!" he cried, through the key-hole.

"Oh, dear!" replied the voice. "Please wait. I shall not be out for some time yet."

"Are you not ready yet?" cried the impatient official. "Why, my dear madam, the vessel is alongside the pier, and everybody going ashore. How long will you be?"

"Half-an-hour."

With a gesture of vexation, the candidate for matrimonial honours set off to pace the deck. The people were now crowding ashore, and the confusion was immense. In the midst of it Sir Benjamin Peakman emerged from the companion hatch

on the starboard side.   He instantly recognised the
auditor-general.

"You here, Freemantle!"

"Yes," replied the other, simpering, and pointing
to the door of the purser's cabin.   "I have come
to meet Mrs. Belldoran.   You must have seen her.
You may perhaps have heard.   We are to be married.   My sister has accompanied me down to meet
her."

"To be married!" cried the knight, gasping with
surprise.   "Her former name was Corcoran!"

"Yes—a vile rascal—there was a divorce—entire
separation.   I hope to make her happy."

"Well, Freemantle," said the knight, looking
curiously into the excited face of his friend, and with
his own features burnished all over with a peculiar
smile, "my impression is that you had better
arrange quietly to go home with me, and say
nothing about it."

"What do you mean?"

" Her former husband, Corcoran, is on board."

" The —— "

" No—excuse me—Corcoran. And from what I have heard and seen, I believe they have made it up."

Freemantle's face coloured with rage.

"Am I to understand, Sir Benjamin, on your honour as a gentleman, that what you tell me is true and *bonâ fide ?* "

" Yes. To the best of my belief ! "

Freemantle rushed to the door of the purser's cabin.

" Let me in ! " he cried, as he thundered on the heavy teak panel. There was a faint scream from within. He continued to hammer on the door, in spite of the knight's entreaties.

"I *will* know all about it," he cried, foaming with rage.

The door suddenly opened, and Mrs. McGowkie stood before him. There was no one else within.

"What do you want, sir?" she said, with all the gravity she could assume.

The knight smiled.

"Why!" gasped the unhappy man, "I thought this was the room of Mrs. Belldoran. I—I beg your pardon. I have made a mistake."

It was at this moment that Lord Pendlebury returned upon the scene. Mrs. McGowkie looked very sad and uncomfortable.

"May I ask," said the peer to Sir Benjamin, "whether this is Mr. Freemantle?"

The knight introduced them. The official, however, was in too great a rage to care even for such an introduction.

"Forgive me," he said. "I must see this rascal at once, wherever he is. I have been grossly deluded."

"Do you mean Mr. Corcoran?" said Lord Pendlebury. "Pray come with me. He has occupied the captain's cabin."

The three gentlemen entered the cabin, where Lord Pendlebury, spinning out the yarn as long he could, described to Mr. Freemantle what had taken place. The expectant bridegroom's wrath was natural, and naturally extreme. He sat down and covered his face with his hands.

"A thousand a year!" he murmured, in his anguish. "I could have retired comfortably on that and my pension!"

Lord Pendlebury glanced at the knight, who was smiling benignly. The astute millionaire loved to see human nature uncovering itself, and he was just the man to offer consolation to such a character in such an emergency.

"Come, come! Mr. Freemantle," he said, half maliciously, half kindly. "You have not lost so much after all. If that is your real point of view, we can arrange for you a more advantageous *parti* than that, in Quebec, I dare say. You shall spend your Christmas—and intended honeymoon—with us at

Oak Park, and Lady Peakman will be delighted, I am sure, if she can send you back to Ottawa with something better than you came for."

The young peer, whose face had worn a curiously mingled expression of regret and amusement, had listened attentively to Mr. Freemantle's objurgations. But when the latter incautiously avowed his mercenary motives, Lord Pendlebury without further parley excused himself to the knight, and after giving Mr. Freemantle, in as handsome terms as he could conceive, Mr. Corcoran's message, he left the cabin and ran to find Mrs. McGowkie. She was on the point of going ashore, with the governess and the phlegmatic Sandy. Lord Pendlebury shook her hand warmly.

"It is all right, my dear madam," he cried. "You need not distress yourself in the least about the part you have played. I have seen the man. He is not hurt. It was not an affair of the heart, but of the pocket. He will soon recover of that.

I have left a millionaire consoling him. Hurra! We can eat our Christmas dinner with a clear conscience."

And so, my reader, I trust may you, and "good digestion wait on appetite."

www.ingramcontent.com/pod-product-compliance
Lightning Source LLC
Chambersburg PA
CBHW020352030726
47496CB00007B/2113